MARIPOSA LANDING

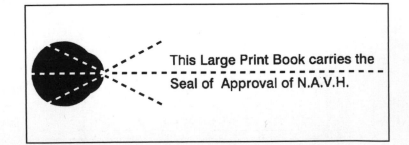

This Large Print Book carries the
Seal of Approval of N.A.V.H.

MARIPOSA LANDING

MARGARET NAVA

THORNDIKE PRESS
A part of Gale, Cengage Learning

Detroit • New York • San Francisco • New Haven, Conn • Waterville, Maine • London

GALE
CENGAGE Learning·

Copyright © 2010 by Margaret Nava.
Angela Dunn Series.
Thorndike Press, a part of Gale, Cengage Learning.

Thorndike Press® Large Print Clean Reads.
The text of this Large Print edition is unabridged.
Other aspects of the book may vary from the original edition.
Set in 16 pt. Plantin.

LIBRARY OF CONGRESS CATALOGING-IN-PUBLICATION DATA

Nava, Margaret M., 1942–
    Mariposa landing / by Margaret Nava. — Large print ed.
    p. cm. — (Angela Dunn series) (Thorndike Press large print clean reads)
    ISBN 978-1-4104-4671-8 (hardcover) — ISBN 1-4104-4671-9 (hardcover)
    1. Large type books. 2. Older women—Fiction. 3. Retirement communities—Fiction. 4. Florida—Fiction. I. Title.
    PS3614.A925M37 2012
    813'.6—dc23   2011047454

Published in 2012 by arrangement with BelleBooks, Inc.

Printed in the United States of America
1 2 3 4 5 6 7 16 15 14 13 12

To Brad . . . my dear friend,
personal hero and inspiration.

CHAPTER 1
FRIENDS

Storm clouds filled the December sky as Angela Fontero struggled to close her suitcase. "Why won't this thing shut?" She sat on the case and bounced up and down.

Her husband, Gilberto, leaned against the doorjamb of their upstairs bedroom and grinned. "Maybe you are trying to put too many clothes into it."

"But I don't know what to take. I've never been to Alabama. What's the weather like this time of year? Is it hot or cold? And what if we go out for dinner? Will we have to dress up?"

Gilberto stepped into the room. "Do not worry amore. I am sure there are many stores in Alabama. If you are in need of anything, I will buy it for you."

"You're probably right. It's just that I want everything to be perfect when I meet Rebecca." Angela's voice trailed off as she stopped bouncing and looked out the window. It had been less than a month since Gilberto told her that he'd tracked down the child she'd given up at birth. The girl was living in Alabama, running some kind of work camp, and Angela and Gilberto were going down to meet her. What was she getting herself into? What could she possibly say to the girl? *I'm sorry I gave you up?*

As if sensing her concern, Gilberto tried to reassure her. "Your daughter will love you, Angela. Just as I do."

Angela jumped off the suitcase and ran to Gilberto's waiting arms. "What did I ever do to deserve such a wonderful husband?"

Raising Angela's chin, Gilberto gazed into her eyes. Her hair was pulled back into its usual silver ponytail. She'd been promising herself to get it cut, and later that morning she would fulfill that promise. Maybe it wasn't smart getting her hair done just before leaving on an important trip, but then maybe a new look would give her strength for what lay ahead. She tilted her head and kissed Gilberto's fingers. "I love you," she whispered.

"And I love you," replied Gilberto. "Now you must hurry and finish what you are doing. I will drive you to town so you can become even more beautiful."

Batting her eyelashes like caffeinated

8

safety blinkers, Angela struck a pose. "Maybe I should get one of those pixie cuts." Swinging the ponytail over her shoulder, she slowly raked her fingers through its silvery strands. "Or maybe not."

Gilberto chuckled. "Whatever you decide is fine, but please, we must leave soon. I promised Miss Gelah I would stop at her house this morning. She has something for you to take to Alabama."

"Really?" Until a couple of months ago, Gelah Spears had been one of Angela's dearest friends. In fact, she was the first friend Angela had made after moving to West Virginia. The two women spent time at each other's homes, shared recipes and gardening tips, and talked on the phone almost every day. Gelah faithfully attended Steve and Monica's church every Sunday, and even provided several able bodies when the church needed painting. But when Gilberto started spending time with the older woman, Angela became suspicious. She'd lost her first husband to another woman and was worried she might lose her second the same way.

Unable to confront either her husband or her friend, she'd let her suspicions eat at her heart until the horrible day when her world turned upside down at the diner.

After that, everything happened so fast she hadn't had time to think. There was the trip to the hospital, her friend Katherine dropping the bomb that she and her husband were moving to Cuba, her brother Tony's visit, and the disastrous church fire. But, as someone once said, things — especially bad things — have a way of working themselves out. And so they did.

Angela's health issues turned into nothing more than a scare, Katherine discovered she absolutely adored Cuban cigars, Tony had entered rehab, and the church was being rebuilt. As for Gilberto, it turned out he was only spending time with Gelah so he could track down the child Angela had given up more than forty years earlier.

Now, because of her husband's association with Gelah, Angela knew her child's name was Rebecca Taylor, and she was getting ready to go to Alabama to meet her daughter. The only loose end in her life was making amends to Gelah. But how could she face her friend after all the bad thoughts she had about her? Just the fact that she had suspected Gelah of being the type of woman capable of stealing someone else's husband, made Angela feel ashamed. When she was a kid and had done something bad, she'd crawl under her bed and cry until her

10

father coaxed her out. Maybe that was what her friend was trying to do — coax her out. It had been more than a month since she last talked to Gelah. Maybe she should forget about the hairdresser and go with Gilberto to see Gelah. Good friends were hard to come by . . . it didn't make sense to throw one away.

Gilberto's mouth was moving, but Angela didn't hear a word he was saying. She shook her head. "I'm sorry, Gil. What did you say?"

Gilberto smiled knowingly. "We must hurry. It is beginning to look like rain."

"Oh, great." Angela leaned against the window and craned her neck to look up at the clouds. "The day I finally decide to get my hair done, it has to rain. My hair frizzes when it rains. I'm gonna look like a porcupine."

"Maybe so," replied Gilberto, "but you will be a beautiful porcupine."

"Keep that up, and we won't go anywhere." Angela playfully punched Gilberto's shoulder, and then raced for the stairs. Halfway down, she turned and faced him. "Well, are you coming or what?"

Gilberto smiled. "You forget, Angela. I am not as young as you. It takes me longer to do things."

When Angela married Gilberto, she knew their age difference would eventually become an issue, but for right now, it was something she didn't want to think about. "Excuses, excuses. Now, let's get this show on the road. I've got places to go, and you've got people to see." She grabbed two coats off the hall rack and threw one to Gilberto.

He caught it, put it on and bowed as he opened the door. "After you, my lady."

A steady drizzle peppered Angela's face as she stepped out the back door. Noticing the truck was already running, she sprinted across the gravel driveway and jumped in. It was warm and comfortable in the truck. *Just like Gilberto's love,* she thought. Within seconds, he was sitting beside her.

"Where to first?" he asked.

Once again, Angela thought about going to Gelah's, but decided to wait until after she returned from Alabama. That way she might have good news to share and wouldn't have to spend the entire visit apologizing for her bad behavior. "To the beauty salon, sir. I want to get this thing over with."

"Your wish is my command." Gilberto engaged the clutch, shifted into first gear and started across the ridge. When he reached the main road, he applied more gas and up-shifted through the gears until the truck was moving smoothly through the hollow.

The rain was getting heavier. "What if this turns to snow?" she asked.

"Do not worry," replied Gilberto. "It is not cold enough."

"But what if it gets colder?"

"It will not."

"But what if . . ."

Gilberto frowned. "Do not worry, Angela. Everything is going to be fine."

Angela knew her husband wasn't referring to the weather. They'd been married only a year, but he already knew how her mind worked. He knew she wasn't as worried about the weather as she was the trip. Did he also know she worried that her daughter might not like her? She didn't expect Rebecca to love her, but what if the girl resented Angela and wanted to use their meeting as some sort of revenge? She squeezed Gilberto's hand and held on to it until they reached town. When Gilberto parked in front of the beauty shop, she finally let go. "I probably won't be much longer than an hour. Will that be enough time for you to go to Gelah's and back?"

"Yes," replied Gilberto. "I am sure I will not be gone more than an hour. Shall we meet at the diner?"

Angela wrinkled her nose. "How about the coffee shop? It's closer."

"Yes. Of course." If Gilberto knew Angela never wanted to set foot in that diner again, he didn't show it. "Have you decided what you are going to have done to your hair?"

"Nope. Guess you'll be just as surprised as me." She kissed her husband's cheek and climbed out of the truck. When she reached the beauty shop door, she turned back and waved. Blowing her a kiss, Gilberto checked the traffic then pulled away from the curb. He was on his way to see Gelah, but Angela knew she had nothing to worry about. Everything, and that meant everything, was going to be fine. At least that's what Gilberto said.

Having avoided beauty shops for more than twenty years, Angela was a little nervous. Should she tell the beautician how to cut her hair, or just ask her advice on what to do? What should she talk about? Politics? Dating? Raising goats? How much should she tip the woman? Did people still tip beauticians? Before she had a chance to take her coat off, a Dolly Parton wannabe bounced out of the back room.

"Well, howdy," squealed the bouffanted woman. "You must be Angela."

Looking around the shop, Angela realized she and the woman were alone. "Ah — yes, I am."

"Glad ta meetcha, Angela. My name's Nadine. I'll be doin' yur hair taday."

Nadine pointed to an empty styling chair. There were two other chairs in the shop, but both were occupied by satin pillows and stuffed Teddy Bears dressed in Elvis costumes. Even though it was the only beauty shop in town, business didn't seem to be booming.

"So what's it gonna be?" asked Nadine. "A cut, a perm, coloring? You'd look great as a blonde. Wanna give it a try?"

Angela shook her head. "I'm going on a trip and don't want to do anything too drastic. Maybe just a trim?" If she had been honest with the woman, she would have told her she'd changed her mind and wanted to leave. Immediately.

"A trip, huh? Where ya going?"

"Alabama."

"Vacation or vistin' relatives?"

Angela considered her answer. "Both really. My husband and I will be celebrating our first anniversary with my daughter who lives there." It felt strange saying the words *my daughter.* How long would it take to get used to it?

"Well, great. How 'bout a French braid? I could weave in some dark extensions to fill it out, and you could dress it up with flowers and bows for your anniversary party. You'd look fantastic." Nadine giggled.

"Gee, I don't know," said Angela. "Aren't braids a lot of work to take care of?"

Nadine removed Angela's scrunchee and ran a comb through her hair. "Nope. All's ya need is a little hairspray and maybe a bobby pin or two."

"Will you have to do much cutting?" The last time Angela took scissors to her hair, the ends had developed lives of their own and stuck sideways out of her head, like straight pins in a red velvet pincushion.

"Nothin' drastic. Maybe jist a few split ends."

Angela knew the trip was going to be stressful. Not having to worry about her hair would make it easier, and not having her ponytail cut off would be a real plus. It wasn't that she particularly liked the way her ponytail looked, because truth be known, sometimes it looked pretty shabby. It was just that she never had to think about it or fuss with it. It was always . . . there. She'd grown used to it, and somehow it helped define who she was. A braid would be a good change. If she ended up not liking it, all she'd have to do was unravel it. What could be simpler?

"Okay. Let's do it," she proclaimed.

Nadine washed and blow-dried Angela's hair, applied pink setting gel, and divided a fistful of hair into three segments. Starting from the top down, she crossed and criss-crossed the segments, added more hair, both natural and synthetic, and pulled tight enough to jerk Angela's head backwards. As she worked, she told Angela about her husband and kids, the trouble she was having with her in-laws, and what she was planning to make for dinner. She even talked about the latest scandal in town — a local teenager was caught shoplifting at a gas station.

"Can you imagine that? A gas station of all places. If I was ever gonna shoplift, I'd pick someplace like the Dollar Store, where there's a better selection of merchandise."

Forty minutes later, Nadine handed Angela a mirror and swung the styling chair around so Angela could view the back of her head.

Angela gasped. "Wow. How'd you do that?" While holding the mirror in one hand, she raised the other and felt the braid. It was tight and solid.

"Go ahead, give her a wiggle," urged

Nadine. "She ain't gonna move."

Angela did as instructed. The braid didn't budge. "Can I sleep on it?" she asked.

"Sure thing, but I wouldn't try swimming with it. That synthetic hair'll shrink up so fast it'll feel like a corkscrew's drilling inta yur scalp."

Angela lowered the mirror and faced the beautician. "Really?"

"Nah," giggled Nadine. "I was jist funnin' ya. But try not ta git it too wet. If it tangles, it kin be a real bear to undo."

"Thanks, I'll remember." Angela was so pleased she twirled the chair around for another glimpse. Although the synthetic hair was a shade darker than her own, it didn't look artificial or out of place. "What do I owe you?" she asked.

"How's twenty fer the do and ten fer the extree hair?"

"That's all?" Angela remembered having her hair done once in Indiana and paying almost three times what Nadine was asking. Of course, that was in Indianapolis, and the beautician was a friend of her ex-husband. Maybe that had something to do with it.

"Yeah," said Nadine. "I didn' do much mor'an wash it. And if you've a mind ta bring the fake hair back, I'll give ya a refund."

After thanking and tipping the woman, Angela stepped out of the shop. It was still raining, so she dug out the packaged rain bonnet she kept in her coat pocket for just such an occasion. The small square package had never been opened, and over the years, some of the plastic panels had fused together. Quickly discarding the useless bonnet in a nearby trash barrel, she pulled her coat collar over her head and made a mad dash for the coffee shop. Once inside, she removed her coat, hung it on an empty coat hook and looked around. Gilberto was sitting in one of the side booths. A woman sat across from him. It was Gelah.

Angela's heart sank to her knees. The last time she'd seen Gelah was in the diner with Gilberto. Now here she was in the coffee shop . . . again with Gilberto. They weren't holding hands this time, but the similarities were too much for Angela to bear. She wanted to jump in the truck and drive home, but Gilberto had the keys. Besides, she'd never driven the dirt road leading to the ridge in the rain, and today was not the day to try it. She took a deep breath, straightened her back and walked slowly toward the booth.

Gilberto saw Angela coming and rose to meet her. Kissing her cheek, he whispered he was glad she hadn't gotten her hair cut, and moved aside so she could slide into the booth.

Gelah pushed a flat ribbon-tied box across the table. "I hope you don't mind my coming, Angela. I wanted to give this to you in person."

There were so many things Angela needed to say, but she couldn't get the words out. Trying to keep her hands from shaking, she reached for the box, untied the ribbon and lifted the lid. When she looked inside and saw a round doily, she was confused.

Gelah reached across the table and touched Angela's hand. "When we first met, I could see you had a lot of love in your heart — for your husband, your friends Steve and Monica, and also for someone you were keeping secret, someone who may have caused you pain. At the time I thought it was a lost love, but when I found out it was the daughter you'd given up, I knew I had to help you find her."

Unable to move, speak, or blink her eyelids, Angela was overwhelmed by Gelah's openness. She'd always wanted to ask Gilberto what had gone on between him and Gelah, but she never had. Maybe it was the fear of hearing something she didn't want to hear. Maybe it was her old belief

20

that what she didn't know couldn't hurt her.

"Gilberto drove me around to adoption agencies, public information offices and libraries. We searched old records, hired a private investigator, and got a couple of my foster kids to dig around in some adoptee internet networks they know about. Gilberto wanted to tell you what we were doing, but I worried you'd be heartbroken if we couldn't find your child. I knew you were upset that we were spending so much time together, but it was necessary. When you saw us in the diner that day, I'd just told him your daughter had been located. Now you're going to meet her. Someone, I think it was Elton John, wrote a song about the circle of life. He said the circle of life moves us through despair and hope, through faith and love, until we find our place on the unwinding path."

Fighting back tears, Angela gently stroked the doily. "Is that what this is? The circle of life?"

"Yes," replied Gelah. "I have always believed that if you have faith and follow your heart on life's path, you will discover that no matter what happens, everything remains connected. You, Gilberto, your daughter, and me. We are all connected."

Angela's tears finally broke loose. "Did

you make this?"

Gelah reached in her purse and pulled out another box. "Yes. That one is for you and this one is for your daughter."

Angela stood up, leaned across the table and hugged Gelah. She didn't care if everyone in the coffee shop stared. She didn't care if they snickered. It felt good to have her friend back in her life.

CHAPTER 2
STAPLETON

A sign at the entrance to the USS Alabama Battleship Memorial Park said the park closed promptly at four o'clock — the digital clock on the car dashboard registered four-seventeen.

"Maybe we can come back tomorrow," suggested Gilberto.

Neither agreeing nor disagreeing with her husband, Angela nodded silently. Even though it would have been interesting to tour the battleship, at the moment, she was only concerned with what was going to happen later that evening. All of the arrangements for the trip — the hotel, the meeting place, even the dinner reservations — had been finalized by a travel agent. That could mean one of two things: either Rebecca Taylor was an extremely busy woman, or she really wasn't eager to meet her birth mother.

Gilberto maneuvered the car out of the museum's parking lot and headed south along the eastern shore of Mobile Bay. The road was lined with reddish-brown pine trees, some as tall as fifty feet and as broad as three feet across. A manicured parkway divided northbound from southbound traffic. There was no sign of litter, garbage or weeds. Everything looked so pristine. Angela rolled down her window. Even the air smelled clean. They were only 800 hundred miles from West Virginia, but it felt as if they'd been transported to a different world — a strange, unpredictable world.

They passed through several small towns before seeing the sign for Stapleton. "Five more miles," declared Gilberto.

Angela nodded again. She wished she hadn't given up smoking all those years ago. She'd kicked the habit right after her divorce from Carl, her first husband. It seemed like such a good idea at the time — now she wasn't so sure. She opened the glove compartment and started rummaging around.

"What are you looking for?" asked Gilberto.

"I don't know," mumbled Angela. "Candy. Gum. Anything." Finding a long-forgotten cough drop, she removed the wrapper and popped it into her mouth. It was stale and chalky, but there was enough menthol left to make her search seem almost worthwhile.

As they pulled into Stapleton, Angela was stunned. Fully expecting to find something similar to West Virginia, she was amazed at how the homes in this small town resembled the palatial mansions in Hollywood movies. Almost without exception, the large white houses lining both sides of the road were boxy and symmetrical with hipped roofs, evenly spaced windows, and large, wrap-around porches. Recalling the power and idealism of wealthy landowners in the American South prior to the Civil War, stately Greek pillars flanked the double-doored central entrances. Angela tried to remember what they called that type of architecture. Antebellum? Yes, that was it, antebellum. But was antebellum an architectural style or a period? She wasn't sure.

The downtown area of the town was a gathering of quaint boutiques and antique shops interspersed with museums, restaurants, churches, and a gourmet cheese and wine purveyor's shop. Angela considered asking Gilberto to stop so she could pick up some wine and cheese for Rebecca, but quickly changed her mind. What if Rebecca didn't approve of drinking?

The road suddenly dipped, revealing a large harbor filled with outrigger fishing trawlers and sleek yachts. A long wooden pier, seeming to point the way to the great unknown, extended far beyond the boats. Halfway down the pier, an elderly man slowly cast a six-foot-wide net into the choppy water.

"This place is beautiful," exclaimed Angela.

"Sì, it is," agreed Gilberto. "I hope we will have time to see it all."

Angela held her breath. Ever since Gilberto announced he'd found Rebecca, Angela had looked forward to meeting her daughter. Now she wasn't so sure. What if Rebecca held a grudge because she'd been given up for adoption? What if she planned to use the meeting to give Angela a piece of her mind? Even worse, what if she refused to see Angela?

Instead of stopping at the pier, Gilberto made a sharp left turn and continued out of town. Almost immediately, the scenery changed. Now, instead of grand old southern mansions, most of the homes on this road were modest cottages and bungalows. A child's Big Wheel sat unattended in one yard; a flat-bottomed Jon boat leaned against a tree in another. Obviously a working-class neighborhood, Angela wondered if this was where her daughter lived.

The cottages gave way to a dense forest,

and as Gilberto sped along the road, Angela peered through the trees hoping for a glimpse of the bay. Even though she'd only lived in Florida for a year, she'd grown accustomed to being near water. There was something soothing, almost therapeutic, about large bodies of water. They seemed able to wash cares away. The river that ran through Steve and Monica's farm was nice, but except when it rained, was little more than a trickle. Nothing like an ocean or a bay. Raising a thumb to her mouth, she nibbled at an imaginary hangnail. Then she saw the hotel.

Set at the end of a tree-lined lane, the main part of the hotel was a white, two-story structure with green shutters and a simple slant-roofed portico. Off to one side stood a reception area, and to the rear, a scattering of outbuildings, barns, and other small structures. Carefully pruned roses whispered a promise of summer beauty. From what she'd read in the hotel's brochure, Angela knew the hotel was more than one hundred and fifty years old and had started life as a cotton plantation. When the Civil War marched across the South, the plantation was converted into a military training center and later into a hospital. Slaves had once lived here in shanties, and

Confederate soldiers had died and were buried in a cemetery somewhere on the grounds. Over the years, several hurricanes and fires had threatened the historic building, but local preservationists had managed to keep it alive.

Gilberto parked the car and hurried around to open Angela's door, but she was already out. They'd spent the previous night in northern Alabama, but without their dog Gizmo along, they hadn't made any rest stops since morning. Angela arched her arms over her head and stretched. One of her shoulders popped. "Wow, that's been bugging me since Birmingham."

Gilberto looked concerned. "You should have said something. I would have stopped the car."

Angela smiled. "Thank you, darling, but I wanted to get here early enough to get ready for tonight."

"What is there to do?" Gilberto's concern was replaced with confusion.

"I want to take a nice long bath, get my clothes ready, do my nails . . . you know, all the things women do to make themselves beautiful."

Placing his arm around Angela's waist, Gilberto steered her toward the hotel's reception area. "You do not need any of those things, amore. You are already beautiful."

Angela leaned into Gilberto's shoulder and sighed. Even after a year of marriage, her husband's sweet nothings were like music to her ears. She felt blessed to have found such a loving, considerate man.

A distinguished-looking man dressed in a black morning coat and white gloves tipped his braid-trimmed top hat and opened the front door. "Welcome to Bayview Manor. My name is Braxton. Please call on me if you are in need of any assistance."

Gilberto and Angela thanked the man and stepped into the lobby. Rather than glass and brass like many contemporary hotels, the Bayview was furnished in antiques and paisley-upholstered wingback chairs. Okra-green walls provided the perfect backdrop for the Spanish Oak banister delineating the stairway to the second floor. Almost inconspicuous potted plants graced highly polished writing tables and lace-covered windowsills. On the far side of the lobby, a Noble Fir decorated with white lace angels and silver ornaments stood patiently awaiting Christmas. Stacks of stylishly wrapped packages sat beneath the tree.

Still leaning against Gilberto, Angela whispered in his ear. "I think I've died and gone to heaven."

A young man smiled broadly from behind the front desk. "Welcome to Bayview Manor. You must be Mr. and Mrs. Fontero."

"Yes," replied Gilberto. "How did you know?"

"Mrs. Miller called about an hour ago and asked if you had arrived yet."

Angela snapped to attention. "Monica called? Is something wrong?"

The desk clerk opened a leather-bound guest book and offered Gilberto a gold pen. "She said to tell you the goats are doing fine, but someone named Gizmo is eating her out of house and home. She also mentioned you were celebrating your first wedding anniversary. I hope you don't mind, I have upgraded your reservation to the honeymoon suite. No extra charge, of course."

Gilberto and Angela turned to each other, smiled, and laughed. "We don't mind."

"Wonderful." The young man retrieved a large pewter key from behind the desk and handed it to the doorman who stood waiting. "Braxton will show you to your rooms. I hope you will enjoy your stay, and if you need anything at all, please don't hesitate to call. There is someone at the desk at all times."

"Thank you," replied Gilberto.

Angela giggled as she and Gilberto followed Braxton up the stairs. "Can you believe it? The honeymoon suite." When the doorman opened the suite doors, her jaw dropped, and she froze in her tracks.

Gilberto gave her a gentle nudge and pushed her into the main room.

A large glass vase holding a bouquet of French tulips, pink roses, white lilies and sprigs of eucalyptus sat on a round marble table just inside the door. Noticing the gift card, Angela removed it from its holder and read it aloud. "Happy Anniversary. All our love, Steve and Monica. Isn't that sweet, Gil?"

Gilberto wandered over to a pair of French doors and peeked through the lace curtains. Without waiting to be told, Braxton unlocked and opened the doors leading to the balcony. Two ladder-back rockers and a small iron table occupied one corner, while a terra cotta planter brimming with fragrant white gardenias filled the other. Down below, a bright green lawn framed winter-bedded gardens and sloped gently to the bay. Two children skipped stones across the surface of the water as their parents watched from beneath a huge live oak tree dripping with Spanish moss.

Angela edged in next to her husband. "Who's winning?" she murmured.

"I do not know." He raised a hand to his forehead and shielded his eyes. "The sun is shining on the water, and it is hard to accurately count the number of times the stones bounce."

Angela was about to suggest sunglasses when the phone rang. Stepping back into the room, she followed the sound and located the telephone on a Queen Anne end table next to a burgundy velvet sofa. Excited that the caller might be her daughter, she grabbed the phone and anxiously said "hello?"

"Good afternoon, Mrs. Fontero. This is Jonathan at the front desk. I'm calling to confirm your dinner reservations for tonight in our dining room. We have you down for seven o'clock. Is that correct?"

Back on the farm, Angela had gotten used to eating dinner early in the evening. Once all the chores were completed and the sun started to set, there really wasn't much else to do except wash up, eat a light meal, and get ready for the next day. *Early to bed and early to rise,* as they always said. But maybe things were different down here. Maybe people in the Deep South spent their evenings socializing and discussing politics. Or maybe the men adjourned to the library for cigars and brandy, while the women demurely worked on needlepoint canvases.

Even though it sounded like a lovely way to while away the time, seven o'clock was five hours off and Angela's stomach was already growling. She needed food. "Seven is fine," she said, "but is there some place close by where we can grab a quick bite?"

"The Shrimp Boat at the end of the pier has seafood and light snacks, and the Tea Room in town serves finger sandwiches and sweet tea. They're both excellent choices."

After driving eight hundred miles, it didn't seem fair to subject Gilberto to finger sandwiches. And what in the world was *sweet tea?* "The Shrimp Boat sounds fine," said Angela. "Do we need reservations?"

"No," replied Jonathan. "The lunch crowd should be gone by now. You'll probably have the whole place to yourself. Ask for a window table . . . if you're lucky, you might even see some dolphins. They like to feed on the small fish that gather beneath the pier."

Gilberto drove back into town and parked in a public parking lot near the pier. The plan was to take a quick walking tour of the town, head back to the pier and get something to eat at the shrimp place. The minute

Angela looked in the first shop window, everything changed.

"Look at that," she screeched. "Katherine would just love that." She pointed at an elegant red-sequined Mardi Gras mask with rhinestone-studded eyeholes, peacock and ostrich plumes, and several long ribbons adorned with delicate silk flowers sitting front and center in the store window.

"What is it?" asked Gilberto

"It's a Mardi Gras mask. People wear them in New Orleans on Fat Tuesday."

"Why?"

Angela knew Gilberto had been to the Mardi Gras several times, but she played along with him. "Because it's fun, silly." Grabbing his arm, she dragged him into the shop. Once inside, they came face-to-face with walls covered in ceramic masks, stick masks and feather masks and tables packed with throw beads, charms and multi-colored doubloons. An overly tall woman wearing a slinky black dress, crawfish-shaped earrings, and a hot pink feather boa slithered toward them.

"Welcome to my shop." The woman's voice was deep and guttural. "My name is Jackleen. Are y'all looking for a gift, or something special for yourself?"

Angela studied the shopkeeper's face. *Was*

that a five o'clock shadow? "A gift," she stammered. "I noticed that red-sequined mask in the window. How much is it?"

"Ahh, yes," crooned the woman. "The Scarlett mask. One of my favorites. It was made by nuns in a cloistered convent in Haiti. I could let you have it for fifty dollars, but I really don't think red is your color, darling. How about something in a cobalt blue?"

"Oh, it's not for me," explained Angela. "It's for my friend Katherine. She belongs to a club called the Foxy Ladies. They're all older women, like me, and they do all sorts of crazy things like going to Key West and ogling all the young rollerbladers." Even though she was wearing long pants, she twisted her leg around so that Jackleen couldn't see her tattoo. "The minute I saw that mask, I knew it was something Katherine would want. She has red hair and wears nothing but red clothes."

Jackleen laughed. "Goodness, gracious. My mother would *love* to meet her. Does she live in Nor'lins?"

"Where?" asked Angela.

"Nor'lins, dear. You know . . . in Lou-Z-Anna where they hold the Mardi Gras. Most people call it New OR'lins or, heaven forgive them, New-or-LEANS. But that is just sooo wrong."

"Are you from . . . Nor'lins?" Angela carefully enunciated each syllable.

"Born and raised," crowed Jackleen. "But when that naughty old hurricane kicked up her heels and flooded everything, I packed up and moved here. It was just as well, really. Competition was starting to get pretty intense down there. Can you believe it? There were five gift emporiums in the same block where I had my shop. A bit much, if you ask me. After all, just how many souvenirs can a tourist buy? Now I own the only Mardi Gras shop within fifty miles, and everyone just loves me." Rearranging her boa, she pointed her Romanesque nose toward the ceiling.

Gilberto muffled a snicker.

Jackleen narrowed her eyes and glared.

Angela pretended not to notice what was going on between her husband and the clerk. "What else do you have in red?" she asked.

Quickly regaining her composure, Jackleen wrapped a hairy arm around Angela's shoulders and led her toward the back of the store. "How about something in wall décor? Or maybe a voodoo doll? One never knows when one might need to cast a spell . . . does one." She glanced over her shoulder and shot another glare at Gilberto.

Gilberto yawned and turned away.

Forty minutes later, Angela and Gilberto left Jackleen's shop carrying the red-sequined Mardi Gras mask, a twelve-inch-tall ceramic jester for Monica, a book about New Orleans cemeteries and churches for Steve, a fleur-de-lis brooch for Gelah, and a cat-shaped voodoo doll for Gizmo. "Do you think I went overboard?" she asked.

"No," replied Gilberto. "But I think Jackleen did."

Angela playfully batted her husband's arm and looked down the street. "Umm, a candy store. Let's go see if they have fudge."

Gilberto followed Angela through the candy store, a dress boutique, two gift shops, and a grandfather clock workshop. When all the clocks in the workshop chimed five, Angela gasped. "Good grief, Gil. Why didn't you tell me it was so late?"

"You seemed to be enjoying yourself," he replied innocently.

"I was, but I've got so much to do. We've got to get back to the hotel."

"Do you want to get something to eat first?"

"No," replied Angela. "We don't have time."

Gilberto shook his head and smiled.

"Whatever pleases you, amore."

When they arrived back at the Bayview, the desk clerk greeted them. "Mrs. Taylor called. I tried to reach you at both the Shrimp Boat and the Tea Room, but nobody had seen you."

"We went shopping," confessed Angela. "Did Mrs. Taylor say if she was still coming to dinner tonight?" The thought that Rebecca might have changed her mind made Angela's head spin.

"Yes," replied Jonathan. "But she asked me to change the reservation from seven o'clock to six. Something about a conflict with her son's schedule."

Rebecca had a son? That was something Angela hadn't even considered. Technically, it meant she was a grandmother. *How could that be?* All of a sudden, she felt very old. Grabbing the edge of the lobby desk, she hung her head and took several long, ragged breaths.

Worried about his wife, Gilberto asked if she was all right.

"I will be," she muttered. "Just get me upstairs. We're running out of time."

CHAPTER 3
REBECCA

With less than an hour to get ready, Angela wrapped her head in a towel and quickly showered. Frantically digging through her suitcase, she considered and rejected a black pantsuit (too stuffy), a Victorian lace blouse (too prim), and a pink angora sweater (too high-school-ish.) That left only a floral peasant dress. She tried it on and looked at her reflection in the floor-length dressing room mirrors. "Not bad," she muttered. "Sort of matronly and mod at the same time."

Gilberto stuck his head inside the dressing room. "Are you ready, amore?"

Angela took a deep breath and turned away from the mirrors. "Yup, let's go."

A classical harpist, draped in a hunter green velvet dress, was performing a hauntingly beautiful sonata in the glass-enclosed conservatory attached to the manor's dining room. The dining room itself was small, about ten tables, and empty, except for three tuxedoed waiters engaged in a hushed conversation off in one corner. Upon observing Angela and Gilberto, one of the waiters separated from the group. "Good evening. My name is Thomas. May I show you to your table?"

Gilberto thanked the young man and placed a hand in the middle of Angela's back. Feeling his hand reassured Angela and gave her confidence. When they reached the table, she smiled at her husband as the waiter pulled out her chair. "Are you sure I look all right?" She ran an anxious hand over her braid, checking for fugitive hairs.

"You are beautiful, Angela." Gilberto reached across the table and laced his fingers with hers.

The waiter presented Gilberto with a cork-covered wine list and explained that the Manor served a "unique selection of award-winning local and imported wines."

Gilberto looked to Angela for a response.

She shook her head. "Let's wait for Rebecca."

"May I bring some coffee?" asked the waiter.

Angela nodded. "Yes, with cream please."

The waiter excused himself, but reappeared seconds later carrying a silver coffee carafe and two gilt-edged bone china coffee cups. Holding the carafe high above the table, he gracefully filled each cup and placed them on the table. Angela added cream to her coffee and took a sip. Even with the cream, the coffee had a robust, almost earthy, taste and smell. "This is wonderful," she uttered. "What kind of coffee is it?"

"Aged Sumatran," replied the waiter. "We roast the beans ourselves." He placed the carafe on the table and glanced away.

Following the young man's eyes, Angela noticed a middle-aged woman standing at the entrance to the dining room. The woman wore chocolate brown palazzo pants, a latte-colored cowl neck sweater, and minimal makeup. Her gray hair was loosely coiled on the top of her head, and delicate gold hoops dangled from her ears.

"I think that's her," whispered Angela.

Gilberto turned and rose from his chair as the woman approached the table.

"Are you Mr. and Mrs. Fontero?" Anticipation flooded Rebecca's hazel eyes.

"Sì, I am Gilberto and this is my wife, Angela."

Angela felt as if she were glued to her chair. The dream of finally meeting her child was coming true. But this was no child — it was a grown woman. With gray hair. Where was her baby?

The waiter pulled a chair out for the woman, but she walked around to the other side of the table and offered both hands, palms up, to Angela. "I am so happy to finally meet you. I'm Rebecca."

Bracing herself against the table, Angela rose and took hold of her daughter's hands. Both women smiled, laughed, broke into tears, and fell into each other's arms.

The waiter leaned toward Gilberto and asked if he was ready to order wine.

Gilberto smiled. "Do you have champagne?"

"Of course," replied the waiter.

"Che Buono. Please bring a bottle of your finest."

"Dom Perignon?"

"Sì," replied Gilberto. "That will do nicely."

Oblivious to everything around them, the reunited mother and daughter continued hugging and whispering in each other's ear, until the startling pop of a champagne cork reminded them they were standing in the middle of a restaurant. Reluctant to let go, they clutched each other's hand as they took their places at the table.

Gilberto raised his glass. "To my cherished wife and her beautiful daughter. May your life together be filled with love and happiness."

Rebecca reached across the table and grasped Gilberto's hand. "Without you, none of this would have happened. Thank you for finding me, Gilberto, and thank you for loving my mother."

Angela fought back tears as she squeezed Rebecca's hand.

"And thank you, Angela, for giving me a good home."

Uncertainty etched Angela's face. "But I didn't . . ."

Rebecca gazed lovingly into her mother's eyes. "You could have gone another way, Angela, but you chose to give me life. I can't even imagine how difficult that must have been for you. Nowadays, being a single mother is perfectly acceptable. Forty years ago, it must have been like wearing a scarlet letter. But you did it, and even though you didn't raise me yourself, you made sure I was taken care of and loved."

Angela hung her head.

"My adoptive parents were good people. They taught me right from wrong, provided me with a good Christian education, and always made sure I cleaned my plate and ate all my vegetables."

Tears began welling up in Angela's eyes,

so she pinched the bridge of her nose to hold them back. "Did you have brothers and sisters?"

"No," replied Rebecca. "My parents couldn't have children of their own, and I was the only one they could afford to adopt." She dug into her pocket, pulled out a handkerchief and handed it to Angela.

Angela studied the handkerchief. It was linen with a delicate scalloped edging and the initials R.A.R. embroidered in one corner. "This is beautiful," she said. "Is it an antique?"

"Sort of," chuckled Rebecca. "My father's mother made it for my baptism. I was Rebecca Romero back then. My parents named me after Rebekah, or Rivka, the headstrong wife of Isaac, who gave birth to Esau and Jacob and became the grandmother of Joseph and his brothers. My grandmother always hoped I would become a nun, but I turned into a tomboy who preferred playing football to going to church on Sunday. I think I was a bit of a disappointment to her."

"I'm sure you weren't." Handing the handkerchief back to Rebecca, Angela blotted her tears with a napkin. "What does the A stand for?"

"Angelita. It means little angel."

Angela knew full well what the name meant, because it was what her father had always called her. Was it possible that Rebecca's parents named their adopted baby girl after her biological mother? "Do your parents live nearby?"

"No," sighed Rebecca. "They died while I was in college."

"What were they like?" asked Angela.

"Simple, quiet people," replied Rebecca. "My father worked in the steel mills in Gary, and my mother stayed home and took care of me. Mom was originally from Mexico and made the world's best tortillas. She and Dad met at a church dinner, and the way my father told it, it was love at first sight. Actually, I think he fell in love with Mom because of her cooking. They got married and bought a two-bedroom prairie-style house in the Cudahee neighborhood in Gary, but when they found out they couldn't have children, they decided to adopt. That's where I came in."

Hungry to learn as much as she could, Angela started asking questions. "What about you? Where did you and your husband meet? What is he like? Tell us about your son."

Taking a deep breath, Rebecca raised her champagne glass and glanced toward the conservatory. Beyond the darkened windows, a shrimp trawler chugged sluggishly toward the dock. Without taking a sip, she lowered the glass to the table. "My husband David and I met in college. He was studying finance and economics, and I was studying social science. I had to quit school when my parents became ill, but David stuck with me. He was there when my mother died, and a year later when my father died. I don't know what I would have done without him."

Angela massaged her daughter's hand. "It must have been hard losing your parents at such an early age. How old were you?"

"Eighteen. I was sixteen when I graduated from high school. David and I were married when I turned twenty."

The waiter discreetly placed three menus on the table and departed without saying a word.

"What docs your husband do?" asked Gilberto.

"He was a banker," replied Rebecca. "After we got married, we moved to Chicago, and he went to work for the Federal Reserve Bank while I finished my degree. Our son, Dominick, was born eight years later."

"Is David still in banking?" asked Angela.

As if in prayer, Rebecca pressed her hands

together and closed her eyes. "He coached high school basketball and was killed in a drive-by shooting after one of the games."

Angela gasped and reached for Gilberto. Her head was reeling, and she seemed to have stopped breathing. In her relatively short life, Rebecca had been through so much. Luckily, she'd always had someone to turn to, someone who loved her. But now that her parents and husband were gone, who did she have?

"During his career, David invested wisely. Some of his investments were transferred to our son's name, others were reinvested or redeemed. I was working with a civil rights group in Chicago when I learned about a Hispanic migrant ministry that was starting up down here. The idea was to provide a safe place for migrant farm workers to live while they were working in nearby fields and orchards. The ministry had already set up a health clinic, but they needed someone to build and run the housing. My father's parents had been immigrants. They came up from Mexico in early spring and picked crops in Florida, Alabama, Louisiana, and Texas. One of the farmers they worked for offered to sell them a house and help them become United States citizens. They lived in that house for fifteen years and had six children. When the Second World War started, my grandfather wanted to be part of the war effort, so he moved the family to Indiana and went to work in the steel mills. They had three more children. My father was the last. I thought working down here would be a wonderful tribute to him and his parents, so I cashed in some of David's investments, bought some land, and the rest, as they say, is history."

The waiter reappeared at the table and stood at attention.

"We haven't even looked at the menus," admitted Angela. "Should we start with appetizers?"

Rebecca checked her watch. "You know, I'm afraid that's all I'll have time for. It's already seven and I have to pick up Dominick at eight."

"Do you have far to go?" asked Gilberto.

"No," replied Rebecca. "He went to a basketball game at the high school. That's less than ten minutes from here."

"Buono," declared Gilberto. "Do you like calamari, Rebecca?"

"Yes, but if you've never had crab claws, you should really try them. The chef here fries them to perfection."

Angela scrunched her nose. "Crab claws? You mean like spiny little pinchers?"

Gilberto grinned. "No, amore, they are called pincers. I had them once in the Keys. They are delizioso."

Angela smiled at the waiter. "Thomas, please bring us a very large plate of fried crab claws and another bottle of champagne."

"No more for me," declared Rebecca. "I'm driving."

The waiter suggested a bottle of sparkling Ariel. "It's nonalcoholic and makes a wonderful accompaniment to crab claws."

"Sì," agreed Gilberto. "That will be fine."

Rebecca turned to Angela. "We've been talking so much about me, what about you? You live on a goat farm . . . right? What's that like?"

Angela chuckled. "Interesting. Before we bought our goats, I never knew they were such intelligent animals. The oldest female herds the younger goats back whenever they get out of the pen, and the male plays with our dog. I don't know if the goat thinks he's a dog, or the dog thinks he's a goat."

The waiter placed a large platter on the table. One side of the platter was filled with crab claws, the other with strange looking golden-brown squares. In the center was a bowl of cocktail sauce.

Angela pointed at the squares. "What are those?"

"They're called alligator bites," replied the waiter. "Compliments of the chef."

Rebecca reached for a crab claw, gripped it between her teeth and pulled the crusty meat from the deep-fried appendage. "How long have you lived in West Virginia?" she asked.

Imitating her daughter, Angela tried one, then another claw. The meat was white and tasted similar to broiled lobster. "Less than a year," she replied. "Gil and I met in Florida when I moved there from Indiana."

"Really? Where in Florida?"

"Outside of Miami. After living in one place for fifteen years, my landlord in Indiana suddenly decided he didn't like dogs anymore, so I had to move because I wasn't about to give up my dog. My brother and his wife live in an over-55 trailer park, and one of their neighbors needed someone to housesit while he was in Africa. I didn't know where else to go, so I went there." Plucking an alligator bite from the tray, Angela dipped it in cocktail sauce and bit into it. Expecting the meat to be tough, she was pleasantly surprised when it ended up tasting like chicken.

"What kind of dog do you have?" asked

Rebecca.

"He's a rescue," replied Angela. "Part Australian cattle dog, but mostly Heinz-57. Someone shot him with a BB gun when he was a puppy, so he's half-blind, but he doesn't let that slow him down. He plays on the teeter-totter with the goats, chases groundhogs down their holes, and goes hunting with Gil. Before I moved to Florida, he was my only friend. Aside from work, I never went anywhere without him. Do you have a dog, Rebecca?"

"Yes," replied Rebecca. "Dominick has a Rottweiler-Shar-Pei mix."

"Wow. I'll bet it's huge."

"It is. I wanted him to get something smaller, but he argued until I finally gave in."

"How old is your son?" Angela did some quick mental calculations. Rebecca was forty-three. If she'd been twenty when she got married, and her son was born eight years later, that would make her grand-son . . .

"Fifteen. He was just eight years old when David died, but he sort of took over as man of the house. He takes care of all the repairs, makes sure my car is properly serviced, and even keeps the checkbook balanced. When I told him I was thinking about moving down here, he contacted a couple of real estate agents and found our property. In the five years we've been living here, he's worked with contractors, plumbers, and zoning inspectors. He's so persuasive, he could talk the spots off a leopard." Rebecca looked at her watch. "I'm sorry, but I really have to run. Dominick worries when I'm late. If you have time tomorrow, maybe you could come by the farm and meet him."

"We'd like that," replied Angela. "What time and how do we get there?"

"Come for lunch. I make a pretty fair andouille and shrimp with mustard sauce, even if I do say so myself. The shrimp are from right here in the bay."

Gilberto's face lit up. "Andouille is a Cajun sausage, is it not?"

"Why, yes," replied Rebecca. "How did you know?"

Angela patted her husband's hand. "Gil was head chef at one of Miami's largest hotels. There isn't much he doesn't know about cooking."

"Oops," laughed Rebecca. "In that case, maybe we'll just order in." Digging into her pocket again, she pulled out a piece of paper and handed it to Gilberto. "Here are directions to the farm. We're easy to find, but if you get lost, just call the number on the bottom. I'll come get you."

Rebecca placed her napkin on the table and rose. Angela did the same. For a brief moment, the two women stood awkwardly facing each other. Suddenly, Rebecca wrapped her arms around her mother and hugged tightly. "I feel like I've always known you, Angela, and maybe I have. Maybe the bonds of motherhood are stronger than anyone realizes. Maybe, no matter what, they can't be broken."

Tears streamed down Angela's face. "I've always loved you, Rebecca."

Rebecca kissed her mother's tear-stained face. "I know," she whispered. Then she turned and hurried away.

Angela collapsed into her chair and blew her nose into the napkin. "I'm gonna have to take this thing upstairs and wash it."

Gilberto laughed and moved his chair closer to Angela's. "I am sure that is not necessary, amore. But if it makes you feel better, we will certainly do that."

"You're right." Angela balled the napkin up and placed it back on the table. "I guess I'm just being silly."

"You are entitled," declared Gilberto.

Angela bit into another alligator cube and frowned. "You know what? These things are great, but suddenly I'm very hungry. Do you think they have anything chocolate?"

Gilberto smiled. "If they do not, I will find a place that does."

Angela kissed her husband's cheek. "L'amo, Gilberto."

"E te'amo, Angelita."

CHAPTER 4
MARIPOSA

"Let's go into town and get some breakfast." Angela stood at the bedroom window drinking her second cup of morning coffee. Dressed in starched jeans and the pink angora sweater, she had combed out the French braid, removed the extensions, and tied her silvery strands into their usual ponytail.

Gilberto looked out the window on the still dark world. "What time is it?"

"It's seven o'clock, sleepy head. Come on . . . get up. We've got a busy day ahead."

Throwing back the covers and swinging his pajama-clad legs over the side of the king-sized bed, Gilberto rubbed his eyes, yawned, and stretched his arms toward the ceiling. Letting out a deep sigh, he asked if there was any coffee left.

Angela pointed toward the nightstand. "Just the way you like it — two creams, no sugar. Now hurry up and get dressed. I want to do some shopping before we go to Rebecca's."

Gilberto raised his coffee cup. "For what?"

"I brought along some old pictures of when I was a child, and thought I'd look for a photo album to put them in. It might make a nice gift for Rebecca. I'd also like to get a little something for Dominick."

Gilberto smiled. "Sì, I will hurry."

An hour later Angela and Gilberto sat at a laminated restaurant table crammed with plates of golden-yellow scrambled eggs, fresh-from-the-oven biscuits, thick-sliced ham, country sausage, hash browns, and soup bowls practically overflowing with grits, red-eye gravy and fried apples. A half-empty jar of apple butter, flanked by equally empty bottles of Georgia peach jam and Tupelo honey, stood center stage.

Not knowing where to begin, Angela groaned and warily eyed the spread. "How are we going to eat all this food? Maybe we should have asked for a menu instead of just ordering the *Special*."

Gilberto nodded. "I am sure they have take-out boxes, Angela. Whatever we do not eat, we can take to Rebecca, and she can give it to one of the families living at the farm."

"Good thought." Angela smeared jam on

a biscuit, shoveled a forkful of egg into her mouth, sampled the ham and sausage, spooned grits onto her plate, and poured gravy over everything. Gilberto watched in amazement. Within fifteen minutes, the grits and apple bowls were empty, Angela's plate was wiped clean, and only one biscuit remained. "Are you going to eat that?" she asked.

"Not if you want it." Gilberto grinned and pushed the surviving biscuit toward his wife. "You must have been very hungry."

"I didn't think so," replied Angela, "but once I started eating I couldn't stop myself. Guess I should have eaten more last night. That hot fudge sundae you ordered was delicious, but it didn't really fill me up. I got up in the middle of the night and checked out the mini-bar, but there weren't any cookies, so I went back to sleep."

Gilberto chuckled and signaled for the waitress. After leaving a generous tip and a tableful of dirty dishes, he paid the bill and held the restaurant door open for Angela. "Where would you like to go first?" he asked.

Looking up and down the street, Angela pointed toward the main part of town. "That way. Maybe there's a bookstore or card shop somewhere down there."

The Pen and Brush Bookstore was filled to the rafters with books, porcelain bric-a-brac, art supplies, children's toys, and a wide selection of greeting cards, calendars, and colorful journals. Angela quickly unearthed a peach-colored, lace-and-ribbon bound album and held it up for Gilberto's approval. "Isn't this gorgeous?"

"Sì," he replied. "But I think Dominick would prefer something a little more masculine."

Angela jabbed her husband's shoulder. "Don't be ridiculous, Gil. This is for Rebecca. I was thinking about getting a book for Dominick."

"But you have not met him. How can you know what he likes?"

"Well . . . he was at a basketball game last night. That must mean he likes sports." Without waiting for a reply, Angela headed for the bookshelves. Finding the sports section, she quickly scanned the titles. There were books about football and baseball (not bad choices), ultimate Frisbee (whatever that was), but none about basketball.

A young woman in a three-piece aubergine pantsuit accented with a colorful animal print scarf, magically appeared. "May I help you?" The woman's voice was melodious, and her words perfectly enunciated.

"Yes," replied Angela. "I'm looking for something for a fifteen-year-old boy."

"What sports does he play?" asked the woman.

Sheepishly shrugging her shoulders, Angela confessed her ignorance. "I'm not sure."

The woman smiled sympathetically. "My sixteen-year-old son just finished reading a novel about two high school boys training for a marathon. He said it taught him a lot about friendship, working together, and never giving up. The book is our choice of the month for young adults. May I show it to you?"

Angela followed the woman to the back of the store where four overstuffed leather chairs sat around a massive coffee table. Two teenage boys with their noses buried in books lounged in the chairs. One of the boys had his feet propped up on the table, but hurriedly lowered them when he saw the purple-suited woman move toward him. A wire rack near the reading alcove contained several books, one of which the woman removed and handed to Angela.

The book's dustcover described the difficulties Brad and James, best friends who were always trying to outdo one another, encountered while training for their first marathon and the impact the race had on their lives. Even if Dominick wasn't interested in running marathons, the friendship aspect of the book might appeal to him. If it didn't, he could probably return the book and find something he liked better. Angela handed the book back to the woman. "I'll take it. Can you gift wrap it, please?"

Back at the inn, Angela spread her collection of photos across the dining table and attempted to put them in order. Her grade school and high school pictures were easy to figure out because they were date stamped on the back, but others were random snapshots, probably taken with a Brownie camera, and gave no indication of date, place, or circumstance. "I have no idea when or where some of these were taken," she complained.

Gilberto sat down beside her. "I will help you."

An hour later, seventy-five photos of Angela in various stages of growth and appearance were securely arranged in the lace-covered album. When the mantel clock above the marble framed fireplace chimed eleven, Angela panicked and jumped up. "Good grief," she shrieked. "Look what time it is. I've got to get ready."

Gilberto placed his hands on Angela's shoulders and gently pushed her back into the chair. "Relax, Angela. We do not need to leave for another half-hour, and you look beautiful the way you are." He gently brushed her cheek and kissed the top of her head.

"But I want everything to be perfect."

"It will be. You will see."

Following Rebecca's detailed directions, Angela and Gilberto arrived at the farm with time to spare. A simple wooden sign at the entrance identified it as Mariposa Landing. Etched across the bottom were the words *Where Everyone is Family.* Trying to hide her nervousness, Angela asked Gilberto what Mariposa meant.

"I believe it is Spanish for butterfly," he replied. "In Italian it would be *farfalla,* but the Spanish version sounds more romantic. Does it not?"

Angela stared out the window. Both sides of the road were bordered with fields of some sort of legume. Beyond the fields were orchards, and straight ahead were houses. Expecting rows of metal Quonset huts, she was surprised to see wood-sided farmhouses surrounded by white picket fences. Inside the fences, chickens pecked at bugs, and hanging from the porches, delicate wind chimes swayed in the breeze. "Are you sure we're in the right place?" she asked.

"Sì," confirmed Gilberto. "Rebecca wrote the name on her map. And look . . . there she is now."

Rebecca waved from the porch of one of the houses. Racing across the yard, she directed Gilberto toward a graveled parking area. The only other vehicle in the lot was a beat up blue pickup truck with some sort of ramp and a beanbag in the bed. Angela wondered if the truck belonged to Rebecca or one of her workers.

Gilberto parked next to the pickup, but before he could circle around to open Angela's door, Rebecca pulled her out of the car and enveloped her in a bear hug.

"I'm so glad you could make it." Like Angela, Rebecca was wearing jeans and a sweater, and also like Angela, her hair was gathered into a ponytail. "Lunch is ready, but I thought you might like to tour the farm first."

"Perfect," replied Angela. "It'll give us a chance to walk off our breakfast."

Rebecca laughed. "I'll bet you went to the White Seagull and ordered the Special."

A puzzled look crossed Angela's face. "How'd you know?"

"It's the best place in town. Dominick and I like to go there after church on Sunday. He's partial to the pecan pancakes."

"What church do you go to?" asked Angela.

"Well . . . ," Rebecca raised her chin and scratched her neck. "I was raised Catholic, but I'll go to whatever church is the closest. Someone, I think it might have been Dolly Parton, once said that God doesn't much care which church you go to as long as you show up."

"So true," chuckled Angela.

Rebecca linked arms with Angela and Gilberto and led them away from the parking area. "See that building over there?" She nodded toward a small white building with a steeple and bell. "That's our school-slash-church. During the winter months, the children go there while their parents are working, and on Sundays a preacher comes in for worship services. Some weeks it's a priest from the Catholic or Episcopal churches, other weeks it might be a Baptist minister or a Methodist pastor. All the churches in town take part in the ecumenical ministry that helps keep this place going. Last winter we even had a Jewish Rabbi, but some people said they had a difficult time understanding him, so I doubt he'll be back. In the summer, we use an old church down on the bay. It's bigger and has huge windows and ceiling fans, so it's a lot cooler and everyone seems to love the smell of the water. Guess it reminds them of home. I'll take you down there after lunch."

"How did you come up with the name *Mariposa Landing*?" asked Gilberto.

"Most of the people who live here are from Mexico or Central America. As I mentioned last night, that was a big part of my reason for coming down here."

"That's right," said Angela. "You said your mother was from Mexico."

"Yes and her parents had been farm workers. My grandmother always loved butterflies, or as she called them, *maripósas.* She painted them on the walls of her house, hung them from the ceilings of her children's bedrooms, and even embroidered them on the mantilla she always wore to church. One day I asked why she liked butterflies so much, and she said it was part of her culture. She told me that when she was a child, millions of butterflies migrated to the town where she lived to spend the winter in the trees. Some had traveled from as far away as Canada. Everyone believed the butterflies were the souls of departed loved ones who came to visit their families. To the villagers, the butterflies symbolized joy, hope, and new beginnings."

"What a beautiful sentiment," said Angela. "Your grandmother must have been a wonderful person."

"She was," replied Rebecca.

"I like butterflies, too." Angela lifted her jeans leg and revealed her butterfly tattoo. "When I moved to Florida, I felt like I didn't have anything to look forward to. I was already in my sixties, I'd been passed over for a promotion, I lost the house I was living in, and I sold everything I owned. I had nothing left, and except for my brother and his wife, no one to turn to. Then I met all these wonderful new people, including Gil, and my whole life changed. One of my friends told me you don't quit playing when you grow old; you grow old when you quit playing. My friend is a little on the crazy side, but she convinced me it wasn't too late to start over again. I guess that made sense because I ended up getting this tattoo. Somehow, it was like a signal that I had changed. It seemed like the right thing to do . . . at least at the time."

"I know what you mean," agreed Rebecca. "I felt the same way. After David died, I thought my life had come to an end. I retreated into a safe little cocoon, and the only person I ever let penetrate that cocoon was Dominick. He showed me there was a whole world out there, one that David would have wanted me to explore. Like your friend, my son convinced me to take a chance and spread my wings. I guess when you start over again you've got to let the whole world know. You used a tattoo. I used a road sign. Do you think it's a coincidence that we both chose butterflies?"

Angela shook her head. "I don't believe in coincidences. I think God has a plan for everything and that everything in the universe is connected. Just like us. You and I may have been separated, but we were never apart. We were still connected by what another friend of mine calls the Circle of Life. Oh my gosh, I almost forgot. She made something special for you. Something that will make sense of all my babbling."

"You're not babbling, Angela. I know exactly what you mean because I've always felt that way, too." Rebecca hugged Angela again.

As if sensing another emotional crying jag, Gilberto quickly changed the subject. "Are all the people who live here migrants?"

"No." Rebecca stepped away from Angela.

"A lot of the families live here year round. They cut alfalfa in the spring and pick pecans and peanuts in the fall. We even grow some of our own crops." She pointed at the fields and orchards. "We've got soybeans along the entrance road and peach trees out back. What the residents don't eat gets sold to some local markets.

"What do the workers do when there are no crops to pick?" asked Gilberto.

"We offer adult literacy classes and vocational training so they can get jobs at some of the local businesses. One of our residents worked at a nearby restaurant while he was studying for his citizenship, and now he owns a sandwich shop in town. You know what they say, 'Give a man a fish and he'll eat for a day, teach him to fish and he'll have food for a lifetime.' "

Even though she had nothing to do with it, Angela was proud of the woman Rebecca had become. She was intelligent, articulate, compassionate, and very much a people person. She had extraordinarily high standards and was obviously doing something worthwhile with her life. She had set goals and seemed to be fulfilling them.

Angela wondered if the child she had given away would have turned out the same if she had raised her. Probably not. Part of the reason she gave her child up in the first place was because she couldn't afford to take care of a baby. She didn't have a good job, the infant's father had denied any responsibility, and her parents wanted no part of an illegitimate child. What had that left? Welfare? No. Her child deserved better than that, and as Rebecca Romero she'd received it. Bittersweet as the truth was, deep in her heart, Angela knew she'd done the right thing all those years ago.

Rebecca continued the tour. "And that barn is where we're going to put the goats."

Angela's eyes snapped open like dry pea pods. "Goats? In Alabama?"

"Yes. We have a big problem with kudzu down here, and someone told me goats would eat anything. I figured I'd give them a try."

Angela laughed. "Left on their own, goats might eat whatever gets in their way, but in captivity, they're pretty fussy eaters."

"Really? What do yours eat?"

"Right now we're giving them dairy feed and hay, but in the summer they graze the fields and get fresh vegetables and scraps from the garden."

"What about kudzu? Does it grow in West Virginia?"

Angela shook her head. "I don't know.

What does it look like?"

"Believe me. If you had it, you'd know. It's an ugly old vine that grows at least a foot a day and covers anything that gets in its way. It devours telephone poles, trees, barns, abandoned houses, even tractor-trailers. Some people call it *the vine that ate the South.*"

Angela laughed loudly. "Good grief. Can't anything be done to stop it?"

"People have tried mowing it, tilling it under, spraying it with herbicides, and burning it, but the roots go so deep nothing seems to faze it."

"What makes you think goats will help?" asked Gilberto.

"A couple of years ago, some goats were set loose in the Missionary Ridge area near Chattanooga, and from what I heard, they ate the vines right down to the ground."

"That is so cool," said Angela. "I'll have to check around the farm and see if we have any."

As they approached Rebecca's house, a teen-aged boy in a wheelchair rolled toward them. The red hoodie he wore did little to conceal his muscular arms. His feet were bare, his dark hair was crew cut short, and his tanned face was set into a huge smile that framed sparkling white teeth. A large brown dog trailed behind.

Rebecca walked up to the young man and hugged his bulging shoulders. "You're just in time for lunch. Did you remember to check the mail?"

The boy blushed. "I'll go do it now."

"It can wait," replied Rebecca. "First, I want you to meet Mr. and Mrs. Fontero. They came down to visit from West Virginia. Mrs. Fontero is my birth mother."

The boy's jaw dropped to his chest as he lurched forward in his chair.

Rebecca smiled and pushed the wheelchair closer to Angela and Gilberto. "And this thunderstruck young man is Dominick . . . my son."

CHAPTER 5
DOMINICK

Dominick glared mischievously at Angela. "So . . . what do I call you? Mrs. Fontero? Angela? Granny?" His dark brown eyes sparkled, and the dimples in his cheeks deepened.

Sensing he was being playful, Angela shrugged her shoulders and retaliated. "Big Mama will do nicely." She could give as good as she got.

Everyone around the table, including Dominick, laughed hysterically. When Gilberto finally caught his breath he asked, "What about *Nonna?* It is Italian for Grandmother."

"Or *Abuelita,*" suggested Rebecca. "It's Spanish."

Dominick scratched his cropped head. "I don't know. Somehow, you don't look like a Big Mama *or* an Abuelita. Can't I just call you Angela?"

Angela smiled. "Of course, but please

don't call me Angie. I'm not particularly fond of nicknames."

"Okay, then," quipped Dominick. "Angie it is." Without finishing his dessert, he pushed himself away from the table and quickly rolled out of the room.

Rebecca rolled her eyes and shook her head. "You know, for as much as I love that boy, sometimes I'd like to shake him."

"Don't worry," chuckled Angela. "He was just teasing." Then dropping her eyes she asked the question that had been nagging her all through lunch. "How long has he been in a wheelchair?"

"All his life," replied Rebecca. "He was born with spina bifida, a birth defect that causes damage to the nerves and spinal cord. He had surgery shortly after he was born, but he was permanently paralyzed and has never walked." Her calm, even tone indicated she had repeated this speech many times.

Angela felt her heart skip. She knew about the disease because a classmate of hers in high school had had it. That girl never graduated. "Couldn't the doctors do anything? Drugs? Therapy? Something?"

"David and I took him to one doctor after another, and they all said the same thing: 'There's no known cure because the damaged nerve tissue can't be replaced or repaired.' They said he would never be independent or able to live alone. One doctor even suggested we place him in a special school for children with disabilities, but when we went to look at the school, we knew it wasn't for him. Or us. Even as an infant, there was something special about him. He was so full of life and energy, we couldn't bring ourselves to just lock him away somewhere and forget about him. We wanted our son to have as normal a life as possible."

Rebecca sipped her coffee and drifted back in time. "We bought him his first wheelchair when he was three and enrolled him in public schools when he was five. Like most kids his age, he cried the first time we left him alone. Of course, it was hard on David and me too, but we knew if Dominick was going to lead a productive life, we had to let go. I guess it worked because now he does pretty much what all the other children do. He rides the school bus, participates in gym classes, and even plays basketball with some of his friends. One time, a boy from a different school wanted to play on the team, but when he saw Dominick he said he wasn't about to play with a cripple. Dominick decked the boy and went on to score more points than any of the other boys. I don't think he knows the meaning of the word *can't.*"

The sound of a barking dog caught everyone's attention.

Rebecca turned in her chair and looked out the dining room window. "See what I mean? He's out there right now trying to climb a tree."

"Is that safe?" A look of concern darkened Angela's face.

"Boomer will let us know if anything happens."

"Who is Boomer?" asked Gilberto.

"Dominick's dog," replied Rebecca. "Those two go everywhere together."

Angela rose from her place at the table and walked to the window. Looking out, she saw Dominick waging war against a three-foot-wide tree. With nothing more than a knotted rope and grappling hook, he aimed at the branches and threw the hook high into the air, obviously hoping to catch a branch. Each time the hook missed its target and crashed to the ground, a monstrous brown dog barked and chased after it. It was a game both dog and master seemed to enjoy.

When the unruly hook pulled down a spindly branch and hit Dominick's head,

Angela panicked. "Shouldn't he be wearing a helmet?"

Rebecca laughed as she turned away from the window. "Yes, but he never listens to me. Would you like to try talking to him?"

Before Angela could answer, Dominick spotted her standing at the window, grabbed the dog by its collar and sped away from the tree. "Now where's he going?" She sounded worried.

"Which way is he headed?" asked Rebecca.

"Toward the parking lot."

"Oh, he's probably going to work on his truck."

"Truck? He doesn't drive, does he?"

"Technically, he's not supposed to because he doesn't have a license, but he jerry-rigged some hand controls, so I let him drive around the farm. He tried driving my car once and nearly ran it into a tree, so now I keep my keys hidden."

Dominick honked the horn as he pulled the blue pickup alongside the house. Leaning across the bench seat, he rolled down the window and yelled, "Hey Angie, wanna go for a ride?" Boomer stuck his head out the open window and barked eagerly.

Almost pleading, Angela raised her eyebrows and turned toward Gilberto and Rebecca.

"Go ahead," sighed Rebecca. "Gilberto and I will stay here and get better acquainted."

"That would be wonderful," exclaimed Gilberto. "Maybe you will even be kind enough to share your andouille and shrimp recipe."

Rebecca grinned. "Only if you share one of your recipes with me."

Like a schoolgirl on her first solo date, Angela dashed out the door and sprinted toward Dominick's truck. Yanking the door open, she shoved Boomer toward the middle of the seat and jumped in. "So where are we going?"

Dominick waited as his grandmother fastened her seatbelt, then said, "There's an old dirt road leading from the back of the farm to the bay. I know some guys down there. Ever been on a shrimp boat?"

"No," admitted Angela. "I was on the African Queen once in Florida and a cruise ship in the Bahamas, but I don't think I've ever been on a shrimp boat. What's it like?"

"You'll see."

Dominick gunned the engine and pulled away from the house while Angela hugged Boomer's neck and held on for dear life. As they raced past the picket-fenced houses, she suggested slowing down.

Dominick snorted. "You sound just like my mom."

Unsure if that was a compliment or put-down, Angela studied Dominick's face. His tanned and shiny forehead was unwrinkled, his eyes deep-set and framed with thick, black, almost feminine, lashes. Coarse stubble accentuated his young jaw. Muscled shoulders sprouted from just below his ears and blossomed into trunk-like, hairy arms. This was her grandson, the son of her daughter. Somewhere inside his body, her blood and genes coursed through his veins. Aside from that cancer scare, she'd never really been sick. But what if she had some sort of recessive gene that had skipped a generation or two? What if one of her genes had caused Dominick's illness? Her dream of finding her daughter had become a re-ality, but she didn't know whether to be thrilled or terrified. She gripped the door handle with her free hand and kept silent until they reached the dirt road.

Dominick slowed the truck to a crawl and turned down the road. "Popped a tire out here last month and went into the ditch. Lucky thing someone came along, otherwise I'd still be there."

"Are we still on farm property?" Angela's voice pulsated with every bump of the washboard road. It was almost as if she were back in West Virginia.

"Nope," muttered Dominick. "And just so you know . . . my mom's never been down here."

Did that mean she wasn't supposed to say anything about being there? And if so, was she being an accomplice to her grandson's covert act or just an unwilling enabler? Either way, she felt uneasy enough to consider telling him to turn back. Then she saw the bay and two round-bottomed boats. Three men waved from the deck of one of the boats. The skeleton of a gangly vine, most likely the notorious kudzu, claimed the hoists and deck of the other.

"Oyé, Domingo," shouted a young, bare-chested man. "Qué pasa, jefe?"

Dominick parked the truck next to the nearest boat and swung his lifeless legs around so he could open the door and retrieve his wheelchair from behind the seat. "No mucho," he shouted back. Without turning to face her, he thumbed a finger at Angela. "Esto es mi abuela."

"Tu abuela?" questioned one of the men. "Es bonita."

Angela was impressed that Dominick

spoke Spanish. It was a language she'd always wanted to learn but never seemed able to master. She'd taken a junior college class and picked up a phrase or two, but not much more. Maybe if she'd paid more attention back then, she might be able to figure out what the men had just said. Hopefully it wasn't anything derogatory.

As if sensing her dilemma, Dominick ordered his friends to speak English. "Ella no habla español, tontos."

"Ah, sì. Sorry." The shirtless man hurriedly tugged a Jimmy Buffett t-shirt over his jet-black hair as Angela climbed out of the truck. Spitting into his hands and slicking his hair back, he addressed Angela. "My name is Juan and over there are Raúl and Miguel." He pointed at the two men who were busy cleaning a fishing net. "Would you like to come on board?"

"Yes, thank you." Angela was grateful the man hadn't offered his hand. She turned to help Dominick, but with his dog close behind, he wheeled away and propelled himself up the gangplank leading to the deck of the boat. Once on board, the man named Raúl offered Dominick a brown paper bag. The boy frowned, shook his head and angrily pushed the bag away.

Juan whipped a tattered rag from his back

pocket and brushed vagrant shrimp parts off the top of a padlocked ice hold. Taking full advantage of the situation, Boomer helped himself to a free meal. "Welcome to our boat, Dominick's granmama. It is nice for you to meet us."

When she first set foot on the boat, Angela felt a little uneasy. Dominick seemed to know the men, but did that mean she could trust them? They looked like some of the pirates she'd seen in those Johnny Depp movies. Maybe they had booty stowed away in that padlocked chest. But when the man named Juan attempted to communicate with her, Angela relaxed. Trying to recall a little from her Spanish 101 class, she whispered, "Tambien, gracias."

Juan's gold-tipped teeth caught the sun as he smiled. "Habla español?"

"Muy poco," she replied. "Muy, muy poco."

Raúl chuckled and offered the same brown bag he'd thrust at Dominick to Angela. Accepting the bag, she realized there was a bottle inside. No wonder Dominick had been so gruff. She removed the bottle's cap and sniffed. "Tequila?"

"No," replied Raúl indignantly. "Es pulque."

Not wishing to offend her hosts, Angela

took a sip. Her eyes watered and her lips puckered as she downed the milky, tart liquid. Taking a deep breath, she forced herself to swallow as she handed the bag back to Raúl.

"No like?" he asked.

"It's good," she stammered. "It's just that I'm not much of a drinker."

Dominick wagged his finger at Angela and snickered. "I'm gonna tell my mom."

Angela's eyes narrowed. "Yeah? Well I'm gonna tell her you drove the truck off the farm."

"You better not," snapped Dominick.

"Watch me." Angela stared at Dominick, grinned, then rubbed the top of his bristly head with her knuckles. The boy grimaced but didn't fight back. Angela loved bantering with her grandson. Even in her wildest dreams, nothing as wonderful as this had ever happened. She wanted the afternoon to go on forever, but noticing the lengthening shadows spreading across the water, she suggested heading back. "Your mother is going to think we got lost."

"You're probably right," agreed Dominick. "Last week I was out after curfew, and she came looking for me."

Raúl frowned. "You have a curfew?"

"Yeah. Bummer, isn't it."

Angela and Dominick said goodbye to the three men and got back into the truck. On the way back to the farm, Angela started asking questions. "Do you like living in Alabama? How are you doing in school? What's your favorite subject? Do you have a girlfriend?"

Dominick reluctantly answered all of Angela's questions. Then he asked one of his own. "Why did you abandon my mother?"

Even though she suspected the subject would eventually come up, Angela wasn't prepared to answer her grandson's question. What could she tell him? Her parents forced her into it? She was too broke? Too afraid? Nothing seemed to justify her action, especially now that she knew everything her daughter and grandson had been through. She should have been there for them but wasn't. What could she do to make it up to them? Was that even possible? Instead of saying anything, she hugged the dog and said nothing for the rest of the ride.

Rebecca and Gilberto were waiting as Dominick pulled up next to Gilberto's truck. "Did you have a nice ride?" asked Rebecca.

"Yes." Angela tried to act cheerful, but Gilberto saw right through her charade.

"Are you all right, amore?" he whispered.

"I'm fine," she fibbed. "I've just got a bit of a headache."

"Would you like to go back to the inn and rest?"

Angela nodded. "Yes, maybe that would be best." She started to say goodbye to Rebecca when she remembered the gifts sitting on the front seat of Gilberto's truck. "Good grief, what's wrong with me? I keep forgetting about the gifts I brought for you and Dominick. Gil, would you mind getting those packages from the truck?"

Gilberto retrieved the packages and handed one to Dominick and two to Rebecca.

"This is so nice," gushed Rebecca, "but we should be giving you presents. Gil tells me you're celebrating your first wedding anniversary."

With all the excitement, Angela had almost forgotten. "That's right, we are." She squeezed Gilberto's hand and gazed lovingly into his eyes. Had it only been a year? It seemed like she had known him her entire life.

"If you're still in town, I'd like to take the two of you out for dinner tomorrow night. There's a fabulous French restaurant up the road that serves fresh-caught fish and a

Chateaubriand that literally melts in your mouth. Rumor has it the building used to be a brothel, but I think it was just an old speakeasy. We used to have a lot of them around here."

Angela wasn't ready to leave Stapleton. There were so many things she hadn't seen and so many places she hadn't been. She looked to Gilberto for approval.

"That is most generous," he replied. "But please, let us buy dinner for you and your son."

"No," argued Rebecca. "It will be my treat. After all, I asked you, and the one who asks always pays. Besides, if you don't mind, I'd like to ask a couple of our friends. I'd like them to meet you."

Meeting Rebecca's friends would certainly be nice, but Angela knew it meant she wouldn't have private time with her daughter or grandson. There were questions she needed to ask . . . things she needed to know. She'd had so little time with her daughter and she wanted to answer Dominick's question — as much for his sake as her own. Realizing any time was better than none at all, she reluctantly agreed.

"Great," exclaimed Rebecca. "I'll make reservations and let you know what time to be there." Looking at the two packages in her hands, she added, "And if it's all right with you, I'd like to open these tomorrow night."

"Well, not me." Dominick tore the wrapping from his present and blankly stared at a book cover showing two teenage boys running in a marathon. Sounding more than a little disappointed, he held the book up for Rebecca to see. "Gee, Mom, look . . . a book."

Feeling embarrassed with her obviously inappropriate gift selection, Angela offered to return the book for something more to Dominick's choosing.

"No," he protested. "This is fine. Thanks, Ang . . . ela."

CHAPTER 6
JACK AND VESTA

Rebecca and Dominick were seated at a large table when Angela and Gilberto walked into the Pointe Restaurant. Across from Rebecca sat a man who looked vaguely familiar and a woman, who reminiscent of Angela's friend, Katherine, was dressed head to foot in red — even her feathered hat. If she'd had claws instead of fingers, she could have been mistaken for an enormous lobster.

Rebecca rose and greeted her mother with a hug. "These are our friends, Jack and Vesta Renoux. Jack owns a gift shop in town and Vesta is his mother. I've already told them all about you and Gilberto."

Angela couldn't believe her eyes. The man introduced as Jack was the sales clerk who had sold her the red Mardi Gras mask. But now, instead of a black dress and pink boa, she . . . he . . . wore a three-piece pinstriped suit, a steel-gray silk tie, and a matching pocket square.

Jack pulled out a chair for Angela. "I clean up pretty good, don't I?" he whispered.

Trying to keep from laughing out loud, Angela bit her lower lip and sat down. "It's nice to see you again . . . Jack."

Vesta punched her son's arm. "Don't pay any attention to him, Sugar. His flair for the dramatic catches most people unawares." The woman's words were like molasses dripping from a mason jar. "A voodoo queen cast a spell on him when we lived in New Orleans, and he's never been quite the same."

A look of concern etched with skepticism crossed Angela's face. "You mean like Marie Laveau?"

"Or one just like her," declared Vesta.

Jack squeezed Vesta's shoulder. "Now, mother, you know all that hokum is just for the tourists. Besides, it was the Chicken Man who taught me my craft . . . not some back alley medicine woman with little dolls and grungy gris-gris bags."

Gilberto looked fascinated. "What are gris-gris bags?"

Straightening his shoulders, Jack smiled. "In Nor'lins, white charms are called juju and black charms are called mojo. Gris-gris comes from the French word for grey and it symbolizes a blending of the two. Gris-gris are small cloth or leather bags containing all sorts of things like herbs, oils, charms, bits of bones, hair and nails soaked in perspiration or blood and coated with graveyard dust. Some people carry them around for good luck, others for more Machiavellian purposes."

"Does your Chicken Man use them?" asked Gilberto.

"Yes. But he got most of his power from chickens."

Dominick snickered. "Go ahead, Jack, tell them *everything.*"

"Chicken Man was born in 1937 to a family of Haitian descent who brought him to Nor'lins when he was still an infant. At the age of nine, his grandfather sat him down and told him something that changed his life forever. 'You have the power,' said the old man. 'The power to help people. God shows you things about people you have no other way of knowing, and you can make use of those things to help them.' " Jack scanned the table to make sure he had everyone's interest.

"A short while later, his grandmother told him that he came from a great line of powerful kings. She also told him he had a royal name. From that moment on, the child was no longer called by his given name, he became Prince Ke'eyama."

"Tell 'em about the chickens," shrieked Dominick.

"I'm getting there," replied Jack. "Under the guidance of his grandparents, the young prince grew more powerful every day. He learned about incense and herbs and began to follow a strict diet that had been revealed to him through prayer and meditation. He was shown, he said, that the common chicken was his most powerful totem, and he made chicken an essential part of his daily diet. Whether it was the chicken or something else, the young prince soon learned he could control every aspect of his physical body. He could chew and swallow glass unharmed and he could even eat fire."

Angela moaned loudly.

"He traveled around the world for a while, drumming, dancing, and sacrificing chickens and other small animals to help the people he met. In the 1970s he returned to Nor'lins and witnessed the confusion and madness of the times, brought on, he believed, by the widespread abuse of drugs. He knew he had to do something. But what?"

"What about the chickens?" demanded Dominick.

Ignoring the boy's interruption, Jack continued. "Prince Ke'eyama determined the best way to attract people's attention and gain their trust was by appealing to their thirst for entertainment. He designed an act not only to amaze his audience, but also to win believers to the absolute power of God working through him and his mastery of the voodoo arts."

"The chickens . . ." snarled Dominick.

Jack lowered his head and voice. "The prince performed his act at different nightclubs and bars around the French Quarter and caused a sensation wherever he went. In a show that included sleight of hand, chanting, tribal dancing, and fire eating, he held his audience transfixed. The climax of each show came when he brought a live chicken onstage, and in front of the astonished crowd, bit the bird's head off and drank its blood using the neck as a huge straw. Once that was done, he bit through the rib cage of the dead fowl and ate the chicken raw. That was when people started calling him the *Chicken Man.*"

Angela buried her face in Gilberto's shoulder and groaned.

Dominick chuckled. "Neat, huh."

"Needless to say, many people were put off by the Chicken Man's act, but many others, myself included, came to understand that what appeared to be a man eating a raw chicken really was an act of sacrifice on the part of Prince Ke'eyama on behalf of everyone there. He wanted to stop the flagrant abuse of drugs and this was his only way of doing it. After each show, he'd be inundated with people asking for help to change their evil ways. I was only a teenager at the time, but I knew something important was happening. I wanted to be just like the Chicken Man, so I worked odd jobs, saved what little money I made, went to his performances, hung around backstage, and learned as much as I could."

Almost fearing the answer, Angela ventured another question. "You don't eat live chickens . . . do you?"

A huge grin marched across Jack's face. "Why? Would that be so bad?"

Shuddering at the mental image, Angela's one word response said it all. "Gross."

"My sentiments, exactly," bellowed Vesta. "I told him if he ate one of those chickens and got the beak caught in his throat, I'd pour enough castor oil down his gullet to force that bird out one way or the other. Guess that was enough to scare him, because as far as I know he's never tried it. Isn't that right, Jack?"

Jack nodded like a petulant child. "Yes, mother."

Vesta patted his hand in approval.

"Even though I've never eaten a live chicken, I learned a lot of things from the Chicken Man, the most important being the value of entertainment. We live in very stressful times and entertainment, in whatever form, takes us away from the moment, away from things that cause stress and problems. I studied magic, learned a couple of tricks, and gave free shows for anyone who'd watch. Eventually I got good enough that I started performing at children's parties. I even dressed up like a wizard. The kids loved it, and it helped bring in some needed money. When I graduated from high school, I knew I had to find a better job. I checked out all the restaurants and hotels, but no one was hiring. My mother encouraged me to open a magic shop, and she used all of her savings to get me started." Jack leaned over and kissed his mother's cheek.

She brushed him away.

"Anyway, the magic shop did okay, but nothing to write home about. So I started wearing my wizard costume on special occasions like Halloween, Thanksgiving, and of course Mardi Gras. It helped increase sales. Then one of my friends recommended

I add more lines to my inventory, like incense, candles, and maybe some local art. She also suggested I wear different costumes to draw in more customers. Just like Chicken Man had done."

Angela giggled nervously. "So that dress you wore the other day was just a costume?"

"Well . . . I have to admit I *am* rather partial to the boa, but yes, that whole getup was just one of my many outfits. I also have a gorilla suit, a pirate's costume, a convict uniform, and even a disco mama's sequined pantsuit." Jack stuck his thumbs under the lapels of his pinstriped jacket. "I wear this suit on Saint Valentine's Day. Of course I add patent leather shoes and carry a Tommy gun, but you get the idea. It's as Shakespeare once said, 'All the world's a stage and all the men and women merely players.' Even my mother gets into the act."

Vesta immediately objected. "Quit telling tales, young man. You know I do no such thing."

Jack closed his right eye and raised his left eyebrow. "Really? What about all those red tee-shirts and that ridiculous houndstooth hat you wear?"

"Those are for my men," she snapped.

"What men?" asked Angela. This was getting better and better.

"Vesta is into college football," explained Rebecca.

"Not just college football," retorted Vesta. "*Alabama* college football, if you please."

Rebecca tipped her head. "I stand corrected."

"What's so special about Alabama college football?" asked Gilberto.

Jack shook his head. "Uh-oh, now you've done it."

Vesta straightened her back, took a deep breath and threw back her shoulders. "The University of Alabama's Crimson Tide is one of the most storied and decorated teams in NCAA history. Since beginning play in 1892, they have claimed twelve national championships, and their seven national championships rank second only to Notre Dame's eight. From 1958 to 1982, the team was led by Hall of Fame coach Paul Bear Bryant, who won six national championships. He always wore a houndstooth hat to the games. He was such a wonderful man." She batted her eyelashes and continued before anyone could stop her. "As of 2009, the Auburn University Tigers Football team had seventy-eight winning seasons, thirty-five bowl appearances, twenty-four nine-plus win seasons, eleven undefeated seasons, and ten conference championships. They played in the Southeastern Conference since its inception in 1933 and won six SEC Conference Championships. Since the divisional realignment of the conference in 1992, they won the Western Division title six times, including three trips to the SEC Championship game."

The red-hatted woman leaned back and waited for a comeback. When there was none, she added one final bit of information. "Back in the day I followed the New Orleans Saints, but when we moved to Alabama, I got all fired up about college football. Those young men in their tight-fitting uniforms just seem to have more energy and enthusiasm than the pro players. I wear red tee-shirts and a houndstooth hat in support of the Crimson Tide, but I also wear burnt orange and navy blue in honor of the Tigers. My biggest problem is deciding what to wear when the two teams play each other."

Not knowing how to react, Gilberto turned a quizzical face toward Angela who shrugged and responded with, "Where can I buy one of those red tee-shirts?"

Vesta broke into laughter. "I like this woman," she stated. "She's got spunk."

"Yes," agreed Rebecca, "She's a keeper."

Blushing under the unexpected attention,

Angela quickly changed the subject. "So, how did you all meet each other?"

Jack volunteered. "After Hurricane Katrina wiped us out, Mother and I evacuated to Alabama in hopes of staying with friends in Bayou La Batre. Of course when we got here, we found out our friends were as bad off as we were. A sixteen-foot storm surge had engulfed their entire village and forced shrimp boats and a cargo ship onto the shore. Their house and all their belongings were gone, and they needed someplace to stay just as badly as we did. Someone mentioned a shelter had been set up about fifty miles away in Stapleton, so we made our way across the bay and ended up at Mariposa Landing. That's where we met Rebecca and Dominick."

"Do you live there?" asked Angela.

"We did, but just until we got on our feet," replied Vesta. "Once Jack found a vacant shop in town and got his business going again, he bought us a cottage outside of town. It's small, but it has everything we need and it's close enough to Rebecca's place that I can walk down there while Jack's at work."

"Vesta is one of our volunteers," said Rebecca. "She comes in three days a week and reads to the children in the day care program. Sometimes she dresses up in Jack's costumes and acts out whatever story she's reading. The kids love her."

"Yes," boasted Vesta. "Even those that don't understand what I'm saying."

"You know, I was wondering about that," said Angela. "How do you communicate with people who don't speak English?"

Rebecca smiled. "I was lucky because my parents spoke Spanish around the house, but Dominick didn't learn the language until we moved down here. Now he speaks it better than I do."

Dominick lowered his head and shot a cautionary scowl at Angela. Was he worried she would tell Rebecca about their trip to the shrimp boat?

Angela grinned and turned to her grandson. "Spanish is such a beautiful language . . . isn't it, Dominick?"

Keeping his head lowered, Dominick played with his water glass. "Yeah, whatever. Are we gonna order soon? I'm hungry."

"Don't be so impatient, Dominick," scolded Rebecca. "This is a party for Angela and Gilberto, and we'll order when they are ready."

"Yes," squealed Vesta, "I hear y'all are celebrating your first anniversary. Now isn't that just too sweet? Are you gonna play kissy face later?"

Jack frowned. "Mother, please."

"What? I was just asking . . ."

"It is all right," said Gilberto. "In fact, I cannot think of anything else I would rather do."

For the second time that evening, Angela blushed. "I agree with Dominick. Maybe we should order."

Jack motioned the waiter toward the table. "Garçon, tonight is a very special occasion. We're celebrating the anniversary of our dear friends Angela and Gilberto. What would you recommend?"

The waiter handed out menus, but suggested starting the meal with Salade Niçoise, followed by duck à l'orange served with wild rice and grilled baby asparagus, and finishing off with chocolate fondue and fresh fruit.

Angela groaned. "That's an awful lot of food." She'd hoped for a lighter meal, maybe seafood, but everything sounded so good.

"We're open until midnight," said the waiter. "I can spread out the courses and bring a different wine with each one."

"Excellent," cheered Dominick. "Wine."

Rebecca shook her head. "Not for you, young man. If I'm going to drink tonight, I may need you to drive home."

"Really?"

"We'll see."

The waiter took the order, easy to do since everyone but Dominick agreed on his suggestions. "I'll just have a cheeseburger," stated the boy. "And a Coke."

Taking advantage of a lull in the conversation, Rebecca reached under the table and pulled up the two gifts Angela had given her the day before. "Angela gave these to me yesterday, but I thought it would be nice to open them at the same time she opens hers." She reached under the table again, produced a large tissue-stuffed gift bag, and pushed it across the table toward Angela. "This is for you."

Angela took a deep breath. "Open yours first," she murmured.

Starting with the smallest box, Rebecca carefully removed the ribbon and opened the lid. Her face registered surprise when she looked inside. "Oh . . . how beautiful. Is this the Circle of Life?" She fingered the doily as if it were an antique.

"Yes," replied Angela. ". . . like from the Lion King. A dear friend of mine made it. She says if we follow our hearts along life's path we'll find out that everyone and everything is connected."

"Ah yes, the Lion King . . . *Life's greatest adventure is finding your place in the Circle of Life.* I've always believed that," said Rebecca. "Just like I always believed we'd meet some day."

Angela's eyes welled up but she held back her tears. "Open the other one now."

Rebecca opened the second box and laughed.

"Is something wrong?" Angela wondered if she'd made another bad gift choice.

"No. Look inside your bag."

Angela removed the tissue and pulled out a peach-colored lace-and-ribbon-bound album. "I don't believe this." She laughed.

"I know," chuckled Rebecca. "Two minds with one thought. Must mean we're related or something."

As Angela and Rebecca eagerly looked through their photo albums, Jack stood up and cleared his throat. "I have an announcement to make."

Everyone turned in his direction.

"Mother and I spent a lot of time discussing what might make a nice anniversary gift for Angela and Gilberto. I suggested a lot of things from my shop, but Mother didn't think any of them were good enough.

"No," she said. "The way I see it, there's only one thing good enough for Angela and her husband — football tickets."

Angela squinted and Gilberto rubbed his chin.

"Think about it," insisted Jack. "If we give you season passes to either the Alabama or Auburn home games, you'll have to come back to use them. The only problem is, which team do you want to support?"

For several long seconds, Angela and Gilberto studied each other's face. Then, as if a light bulb had gone off in her head, Angela suggested, "Both. One for Gilberto and one for me. That way we'll each have our own team to root for."

Vesta applauded. "What a wonderful idea. It will give you an excuse to come back twice as often."

"They don't need an excuse," said Rebecca. "They're family."

CHAPTER 7
LEAVING STAPLETON

Even though it was officially winter, the temperature was in the mid-60s. A flock of yellow and black goldfinches flitted through the leafless branches of a red alder, while several people chatted quietly outside the small white building that served as Mariposa Landing's church. If this had been any other day, Angela and Gilberto would have already been on the road, heading back home to West Virginia. However, since it was Sunday, they decided to delay their departure so they could attend services with Rebecca and the people who lived at the farm.

In her mind's eye, Angela envisioned what was happening back home in the hollow. It had been less than a month since the disastrous fire destroyed Steve's church, and services were being held in Pam and J.B. Walton's barn. J.B. had generously moved all his cows out of the building and the slightly scarred pews in — not a totally altruistic gesture considering it was his illegal still that had caused the fire. He'd also built a small altar and what he called a *preacher's perch* from plywood and recycled two-by-fours. Maybe there was hope for the man, after all. Monica would be lighting candles while Steve made last minute changes to his sermon. It was almost Christmas. Would he talk about the astonishing miracle of Christ's birth or the sacrilege of its commercialism?

People would be slowly filing in through the barn doors and taking their seats in the pews. Who was there? Sharon and her family? Gelah? Little Florence? Even though she'd been gone less than a week, Angela realized she was homesick. As much as she didn't want to leave Rebecca and Dominick, she missed Steve, Monica, and of course, the goats. And she felt almost heartsick for Gizmo. He was her buddy, the one who'd stuck with her through good times and bad. He was the one she talked to when no one else would listen. How could she have just gone off and left him alone? She made a mental promise never to let that happen again.

Shaking her head, she forced herself back to Alabama and the little white church. A brown-robed monk stepped from inside the church and encouraged the people standing outside to enter. "Entre por favor. Hay espacio para todos."

Everyone, including Angela and Gilberto, entered and took a seat. The monk was correct — there was room for everyone. In fact, most of the metal folding chairs were empty. It reminded Angela of when Steve and Monica had first invited people to join their church. They'd tried everything they could think of, but nothing happened until Katherine came up with that scatter-brained idea about starting a club like her Foxy Ladies. Of course, trying to talk farm wives into setting their chores aside for an afternoon jaunt was out of the question. Things like that just didn't happen in the hollows. But sewing curtains? Now there was an idea. After one morning of stitching, chatting, and sharing a potluck lunch, several families living in the hollow started attending Steve's services.

Angela wondered if she should ask Katherine to fly in from Cuba. Maybe she could get people to attend Rebecca's church as well. Or, better yet, maybe she should get Vesta to liven things up. Wouldn't that be something? Angela looked around the church for the football fanatic. Like many others, Vesta was absent.

Rebecca slid into the seat next to Angela and kissed her cheek. Reaching out to Gilberto, Rebecca wrapped her fingers around his wrist and squeezed. "I'm so glad you could make it," she said. "Father Gutierrez is one of our favorites."

"Where's Dominick?" whispered Angela.

"Outside," replied Rebecca. "He and the rest of the choir will accompany Father to the altar."

"Choir? You mean he sings?" Realizing she'd spoken too loudly, Angela sheepishly looked around to see if she'd disturbed anyone. Fortunately, she hadn't.

Rebecca smiled and nodded her head. "Like an angel."

A teenage boy carrying a large wooden cross led the way as the monk and seven tennis-shoed choir members filed slowly into the church. The priest and the cross-bearer climbed the two short steps to the altar, while the choir members took their places in the front row. With three seats to each side, Dominick positioned his wheelchair in the middle spot. More worshipers followed the choir and found places to sit. It appeared the church was going to fill up after all.

The priest blessed the congregation and

began the obviously Catholic service with an opening prayer. "Lord God, may we your people, who look forward to the birthday of Christ, experience the joy of salvation and celebrate the coming feast with love and thanksgiving. We ask this through Christ, our Lord, forever and ever . . ."

A quiet "Amen" resonated through the church. It surprised Angela that the Mass wasn't being said in Spanish. After all, that was what most of the farm workers spoke. Maybe praying it in English was one of the ways of helping them assimilate to their new surroundings.

Reading from a paperbound missal, Angela followed the Mass. At one time, she'd known all the prayers by heart. At one time, they'd been important to her. What had happened to change all of that? She couldn't remember why she'd stopped going to church, just that she had. It wasn't until she'd met Steve and Monica in Florida that she realized something was missing in her life. And then, after spending those terrifying hours hiding in a synagogue basement while a hurricane tried to rip the world apart, she'd started attending Steve's services on a regular basis. She'd even gone to a Catholic church a couple of times, but hadn't made it a practice because she didn't think any priest in his right mind would let her back in . . . not after being away for so long.

When it came time for the first reading, a young woman rose, genuflected in front of the altar, and approached the podium. Opening a large red book, she read, "A reading from the book of the prophet Zephaniah." She read about joy and gladness and rejoicing, perfect sentiments for two weeks before Christmas, then she turned toward the choir and signaled for them to take over.

Two girls stepped forward, faced the people in the church and sang the responsorial psalm. "Cry out with joy and gladness for among you is the great and Holy One of Israel." When the girls raised their hands in the air, the congregation repeated their words.

Dominick turned around, and with a songbook on his lap, began chanting. "God indeed is my savior; I am confident and unafraid. My strength and my courage is in the Lord and with joy I will draw water at the fountain of salvation."

Angela closed her eyes and listened. Twice again the girls sang the response and twice again Dominick chanted a verse. His voice was rich and strong, more intense than a baritone but without the dark quality of a bass. When the choir was finished, the young woman on the altar began the second reading. But Angela didn't hear it. Nor did she hear much of the rest of the service. All she heard were Dominick's words. Did he know what he'd said? Did he mean what he'd said?

Here was a young man living with a profound medical condition that should have disabled him from participating in what other people might call a normal life. But Dominick wasn't like other people . . . he was exceptional. He went to school like other children his age, he played basketball, he even drove a truck. From what his mother said, he was a mathematical genius as well as being a shrewd businessman. He had a wonderful sense of humor, he could speak at least two languages, and now he'd shown he could sing. He not only took the lemons life handed him and turned them into lemonade, he made the best lemonade possible. What drove him? His mother? His friends? His faith?

When the priest gave the final blessing and descended from the altar, the choir sang a recessional hymn. Although most of the people started leaving the church, Angela stood where she was. She felt comfortable in the small church and wanted to listen as Dominick and the choir finished their song.

A few minutes later, Dominick rolled his wheelchair down the center aisle and stopped where Angela, Rebecca, and Gilberto were waiting. "Hey . . . everyone ready for pancakes at the White Seagull?"

Clutching her stomach, Angela moaned. "I'm still full from last night. I don't think I could handle that much food. Besides, Gil and I should probably get going. We've got a long ride ahead of us."

Rebecca pouted. "Oh please, can't you stay a little while longer? We could go to the Waffle House out on the four lane and get sausage biscuits. The service there is really fast, and you could just hop on the road when we're finished. Please, please, please?"

Angela laughed. "Now I see where Dominick gets his persuasiveness." She turned to Gilberto. "What do you think, Sweetheart?"

"It is only four hours to Gadsden," replied Gilberto. "If we leave by noon, we will get there before dark. Then it would be less than six hours to home."

"Well, okay then," agreed Angela. "We're off to the Waffle House. Maybe I'll even get some grits and gravy . . . I just love that stuff."

"Thought you said you weren't hungry,"

teased Dominick.

Like most others, Stapleton's Waffle House was a long, narrow structure with yellow tile and an orange, brown, and yellow-striped canopy stretching the full length of the single glass wall. Once inside, Angela, Gilberto, and Rebecca slid into an empty booth, while Dominick parked his wheelchair and wiggled in next to his mother.

Angela quickly scanned the menu. "What? No grits?"

Rebecca laughed. "They don't have to put them on the menu . . . they just set them on the table along with the jam and honey."

"They did that at the coffee shop we went to the other day," observed Gilberto. "Remember, Angela?"

Angela groaned. "How could I forget?"

A waitress wearing a name tag identifying her as *Bitzy* took everyone's order, poured coffee all around, and headed back to the kitchen.

"That's a cute name," remarked Angela.

"Yes," replied Rebecca. "Most of the people in the Deep South have such long names they either shorten them or take nicknames."

"Why is that?" asked Gilberto.

"Southern mothers often name their

children after ancestors," replied Rebecca. "It's almost law. Unfortunately, the more ancestors you have, the longer your child's name. Some poor kids end up with four or five names."

Dominick chuckled. "One of the kids I go to school with goes by the name *Ducky*. When I asked him how he got that name he said he was named after his father, Charles Reginald Hollingswood Quackenbush the third. The kid's father was a bird hunter, so instead of being called Charles Reginald Hollingswood Quackenbush the fourth, the kid became *Ducky*. Of course his dad wasn't real happy at first, but when he realized his son wasn't ridiculing him, he gave in. Sort of."

"Do you have a nickname?" asked Angela.

"Yeah, but my Mom doesn't like it."

Angela faced her daughter. "Why? What is it?"

"Frog," muttered Rebecca.

"That's cute," laughed Angela.

Rebecca shook her head. "No, it isn't. Some smart-aleck kid started calling Dominick that when he saw him bouncing around on the ground without his wheelchair. Sometimes he'll do that when he doesn't want to be bothered with his chair. Anyway, the kid said Dominick looked like a frog. That's not cute — that's mean-spirited."

"Ahh, come on, Mom," objected Dominick. "It's not so bad. You should hear what I call him."

"I don't think I want to," retorted Rebecca.

Changing the subject, Angela asked her grandson where he learned to sing.

"Fourth grade," he replied. "There was this really pretty girl in my class, but she never paid any attention to me. When I found out she signed up for the Christmas pageant, I did too. She got the part of Mary and I ended up being one of the angels. Of course, that meant I had to sing, but it was okay because I got to sit right next to her."

"So, did she pay attention to you after that?"

"No, but one of the other girls did. Her name was Sandra. She had long brown hair and hazel eyes. I thought she was beautiful, and I told her so. After the pageant, she gave me my first kiss. So I guess everything worked out all right."

"Do you date much?" asked Gilberto.

Dominick blushed. "I do my share."

"And what about sports?"

"Mostly just basketball and tennis," he replied. "But I'm thinking about taking up marathon racing."

Angela's jaw dropped. "Marathon racing?"

"Sure," replied Dominick. "Why not? I read that book you gave me, and it got me thinking. So I went online and found out lots of guys like me do it. Some girls, too."

"You read the book? Already?"

"Yeah, it was only three hundred pages."

Angela shook her head in disbelief. "It would take me more than a week to read three hundred pages."

Rebecca patted her son's hand. "What he isn't telling you is that he stayed up all night reading. I tried to get him to put that book down, but he's sort of like a pit bull. Once he locks on to something, he doesn't let go."

"But three hundred pages? In one night?"

"I know. Then he spent half the morning surfing the Internet for wheelchair racing information. It was all I could do to get him to take a nap before dinner last night."

"Wow," exclaimed Angela. "I didn't even know there was such a thing as wheelchair racing."

"Oh yeah," replied Dominick. "They've got these special racing chairs with two large wheels in the back and one small one in the front. They're really cool. If you've got Internet, I could send you some pictures."

"We haven't gotten around to buying a

computer yer," replied Angela. "But I'll bet the library in town has one. Maybe I could sign in there."

"Log on," corrected Dominick.

"What?"

"The term is log on, not sign in."

"Oh, I am sooo . . . sorry."

Bitzy brought the food and everyone dug in. Rebecca and Gilberto had omelets, Angela had a buttermilk waffle covered with sliced peaches, pecans, and whipped cream, and Dominick had the All Star Special — two eggs, six slices of bacon, biscuits and gravy, and a waffle served with hot maple syrup and melted butter. When all the food was eaten and everyone had had their fill of coffee, they walked outside to the cars.

"I wish you could stay longer," sighed Rebecca.

"Me, too," agreed Angela. "But we've got to get back to help Steve and Monica get ready for Christmas services."

"Maybe you could come back for Easter. One of the men dresses up like the Easter bunny and all the ladies wear frilly Sunday bonnets. We even have a big Easter egg hunt for the children. It's lots of fun."

"It sounds like it," said Angela. "But this will be our first kidding season with the goats, and I don't know how much help

Monica is going to need."

"Well, Easter is late this year, so maybe you can take care of the goats and come down here as well. We'd drive up to West Virginia, but I don't know who I would get to run the farm."

"Don't worry," replied Angela. "We'll work something out."

It broke Angela's heart to leave her daughter and grandson. They had only spent a couple of days together but they had already formed a bond. Maybe it was true what Gelah said about everyone being connected. Maybe that was what life was all about — being connected. Maybe that was what made it all worthwhile. She hoped Gelah would get to meet Rebecca and Dominick some day. She deserved to meet them.

Angela and Rebecca shared a last, quick hug while Gilberto and Dominick watched.

Dominick sneered. "Women . . ."

"Yes," agreed Gilberto, "women."

As Gilberto drove away from the Waffle House, Angela leaned out the window and waved goodbye to Rebecca and Dominick. She waved, in fact, until she could no longer make out their faces.

Gilberto urged her to close the window. "We will come back," he assured her.

Angela sighed and did as Gilberto requested. The visit had been so short, and she wondered when she would see her daughter again. "It's just so hard to leave," she moaned.

"I know, but you had a wonderful visit, did you not?"

"Much better than I'd expected," replied Angela. "And Dominick . . . now wasn't he a surprise?"

"Yes. He is a very nice young man."

"I'm glad I bought him that book. Do you think he'll really get into racing?"

"He seems very determined," replied Gilberto.

Angela watched silently as the large white houses, with their wraparound porches and Greek columns, passed by. She watched as the manicured parkway fell far behind. When they reached Battleship Park, she turned to Gilberto. "You know what? I think I know what I'm going to buy Dominick for Christmas."

Gilberto smiled. "I am sure you do, *amoré,* I am sure you do."

CHAPTER 8
BACK AT THE FARM

Monica grinned and pushed a large piece of yellow paper across the table toward Angela. "That's a list of all the things we've got to do this week. I would have done some of them last week, but I didn't want you to miss out on any of the fun." The two friends had just finished the morning milking and were sitting in Monica's kitchen, sharing a well-deserved coffee break.

Angela quickly scanned the list: Trim goats' hooves, pick up enterotoxemia and tetanus vaccines, prepare birthing kit, disinfect kidding stall, buy electric shaver for does' haircuts, get film for Steve's camera, take Gizmo to vet for shots and tranquilizer. "Gizmo's gonna need tranquilizers?"

"You know how he is about those goats. I'm afraid if they start bleating too loudly, he'll panic or something."

"Good thinking," replied Angela. "And

117

while we're at it, maybe we should get some for ourselves."

Monica chuckled. "Don't worry, Pam said she'd come down and give us a hand."

"Really? I didn't know she knew anything about delivering goats."

"She doesn't. Just pigs and cows. But how different can goats be?"

Angela sipped her coffee. "Well, I guess we're gonna find out."

Leaving Rebecca and Dominick in Alabama had been hard on Angela, but coming back to the farm made it a little easier. She was happy to see Steve and Monica, and there were so many things to look forward to. Christmas was around the corner, spring seed catalogs were already filling up the mailbox, and if Bucky had done his duty in September, baby goats would be arriving sometime in early February. Then there was Easter — the celebration of joy, hope, and new beginnings — just like Rebecca's grandmother's butterflies. Angela reached across the table and squeezed Monica's hand. "Have I told you lately how grateful I am to you and Steve and how much I love you both?"

Monica's eyes shone with a strange mixture of disbelief and gratitude. "Wow. What brought that on?"

"I don't know," replied Angela. "It's just that my life has changed so much since I left Indiana, and I think I have you and Steve to thank for a lot of it."

"How so?"

"You welcomed me into your home, you were there the first time I went out with Gil, you were at our wedding, and you gave us a house. You were always . . . there. And you never asked for anything in return."

Tears welled up in Monica's eyes. "And you were there for me, Angela. You defended me when I needed defending, you put up with my crazy mood swings, and you made me look at myself when I didn't want to. You showed me what I was doing wrong, and you helped me find a way to fix it. I've never told you this, but I came very close to losing Steve."

"When?"

"Right after you and Gil moved here. He knew I wasn't happy, and he blamed himself for it. He said he was beginning to think the whole idea of buying the farm and starting a church was a mistake. After all, what did a defrocked priest know about farming?" Monica lowered her head and stared into her coffee cup. "He even suggested that I was unhappy because I left my orders."

"Oh, Monica, I'm so sorry. Why didn't

you tell me sooner?

"You and Gil were so happy, I didn't want to ruin anything for you. Besides, once you talked me into going to the doctor everything changed."

"Really?"

"Well, that and the goats."

Angela smiled and inhaled a sniffle. "You know . . . you've never told me. How did you and Steve get together in the first place?"

Monica nodded and leaned back in her chair. "I went to teach school in Nicaragua and was assigned to Steve's parish. When we found out we were both raised in New England, we immediately became friends. But that's all it ever was . . . just friendship. Nicaragua was a tough place for Catholics because the Church opposed the violent tactics of the Somoza regime. Needless to say, that wasn't a popular stance. When Somoza was overthrown in '79 and the Sandinistas took over the country, things went from bad to worse. Even though the new government promised great reform, it was opposed by rebel groups known as Contras who targeted, kidnapped, and tortured civilians, especially priests and nuns. When my school was torched, I tried to get the children to safety, but we were captured by the rebels and taken prisoner."

Angela gasped and raised a hand to her mouth.

"The Contras locked me and six children up in a small shed. We had no windows, no fresh air, no bathroom. We were given food and water in the morning, but by afternoon, whatever was left was consumed by the rats. It took Steve three days to find us, and when he opened that shed door, I crawled into a corner and cowered."

Not sure if she really wanted an answer, Angela asked Monica if she'd been abused.

Monica shook her head. "No, not physically. But I had been so terrified I couldn't eat or sleep for a week. When I was finally able to sleep, I would wake up screaming. Steve took care of me and made sure I was never alone. He fed me warm soup during the day and slept on the floor by my bed at night. My Mother Superior wanted me to return to the home convent in Baltimore, but I couldn't leave Steve. He made me feel safe . . . and loved."

Angela nodded. She knew the feeling of safety. And love.

"When I told Steve how I felt, he hugged me and I knew that, from then on, we would never be apart."

Angela rose from the table and reached

for Monica. As the women hugged and wept in each other's arms, their husbands entered the room.

"Will you look at that," laughed Steve. "Leave two women alone long enough, and they'll end up crying about something."

Gilberto rushed to Angela's side. "Are you all right, amore?"

"Yes," replied Angela. "We were just telling sad stories."

"Well, save them for later," teased Steve. "Gil and I are going into town and thought you might like to join us. We could even stop and get some lunch."

"Great idea," chirped Angela. "Maybe we can knock a couple things off Monica's list."

"What list?" asked Steve.

"This one." Angela handed the yellow sheet to Steve.

He looked it over and frowned. "You forgot one very important thing."

"What?" asked Monica and Angela in unison.

"Elbow length gloves."

"What on earth for?" asked Monica.

"In case you have to go in after one of the babies."

Angela wrinkled her nose and closed one eye. "Yuk."

"He's right," agreed Monica. "It's one of

the things that's supposed to go in the birthing kit. Guess I better double-check to make sure I didn't miss anything else."

Steve headed for the kitchen door. "Well, hurry up. The bus leaves in ten minutes."

Monica threw a dishtowel in her husband's direction. "You better not leave without us."

"We will wait," shouted Gilberto as he quickly exited the kitchen.

Angela carried the coffee cups to the sink, quickly filled them with water, and turned to Monica. "Do you think Steve would mind dropping me off at the library? I've got some research to do."

"On what?" asked Monica.

"Wheelchair racing."

"Does this have something to do with Dominick?"

"Yes," replied Angela. "I bought him a book about a couple of kids who ran a marathon, and he seemed really interested. Rebecca said he spent a lot of time on the Internet looking for information about wheelchair racing. Thought I could do the same thing. Maybe even check out prices on racing equipment."

"Watch out world," teased Monica, "here comes Gramma Angela."

Angela and Monica slipped into their barn

jackets and bolted out the door. When they reached the truck, Monica jerked the back-door open and shouted, "I get shotgun." Angela slid into the backseat and pouted. "Okay, but it's my turn coming home."

Winter had taken a firm hold on the hollow. It had snowed earlier that morning, but the only tracks on the single-lane road were those of the school bus and a solitary rabbit. A thin layer of ice was beginning to form along the edges of the river, but the deeper center portion ran free and shone like black satin reflecting the slim, bare silhouettes of overhanging trees. A lone deer peeked from behind one of the trees. It had no antlers and, based on its size, Angela assumed it was either a doe or a fawn. What did these beautiful animals eat in winter? Nuts? Berries? Tree bark? With the heavy cover of snow blanketing the ground and shrubs, the deer's choices were probably limited. Maybe she should stop at the co-op and buy some grain or a salt lick. Or maybe she should let the deer forage for itself.

As requested, Steve dropped Angela off at the library. "Will an hour be enough?" he asked.

"Yes," she replied. "I'll just print off a bunch of stuff and take it home to read. If I don't find what I'm looking for, I can always come back next week."

Angela entered the one-story red-bricked building that served as the town's library, genealogy center, and newspaper office. She knew this was one of the places Gilberto and Gelah visited when they were trying to locate Rebecca, but she'd never been here. A large oak door to the right indicated the entrance to the Country Herald Newspaper; a similar door to the left indicated the Genealogy Center. That meant the glass doors straight ahead probably led to the library.

Looking inside, Angela saw a large counter that was either the circulation or reference desk. Maybe both. She entered the room and was surprised at its size. Row after row of metal shelves filled with books patiently awaiting readers flanked both sides of the counter and floor-length windows looked out on deserted lawn furniture. It was good to see the town had such a nice library, but disappointing to find it empty.

A small crystal bell with a sign saying *Please Ring* sat on the counter. Angela picked it up and shook it. A voice from behind the farthest shelves softly proclaimed, "I'll be right there."

When the voice developed into a body, Angela realized both belonged to a woman

Gelah had once brought to Steve's church.

The woman immediately recognized Angela. "You're that good-looking preacher's friend, right?"

Angela smiled. Obviously she wasn't the only one who appreciated Steve's good looks. "Yes, but we haven't seen you in church lately. Have you been well?"

"Oh, lordy, yes," replied the woman. "I only went that one time with Gelah because she wanted me to see the new preacher. We don't get many new people in the hollers, and I like to meet 'em all. My son has a church up on Thompson Ridge, so I'm obliged to go there of a Sunday. Otherwise, he raises the dickens with me."

"I see," chuckled Angela.

"So what brings you to the library?" asked the woman.

Angela scanned the room. "I was hoping to do some Internet research, but I don't see any computers."

"We only have one," stated the woman. "It's back here behind the counter. Come around and pull up a chair. I'll start it up for you, then get out of your way."

"You don't have to leave," objected Angela.

"That's okay, I've got work to finish in the stacks anyway." The woman turned the computer on, clicked on the Internet icon, and true to her word, left Angela alone.

Angela had never been proficient with computers, but she knew the basics. She pulled up a search engine, typed the words *Wheelchair Racing,* and hit the *Enter* button. The computer creaked and groaned but eventually pulled up more than 12 million listings. There was everything from encyclopedia websites to those talking about the basics of wheelchair racing and touting the latest, greatest equipment available. Not sure which to pick, she opened a couple of how-to sites, picked out the pages that interested her and sent them to what she hoped was a printer. Off behind the racks to her right, she heard the machine doing its job. *So far, so good.*

Next, she opened some equipment sites, chose more pages, and sent them to the printer as well. Then, trying some different word combinations, she looked up information about training, techniques, and race schedules. Every few minutes, she walked back to the printer and retrieved her printed documents. After half an hour, she added more paper to the machine. She wondered how much the library lady was going to charge for all the paper she'd used. Checking her pockets, she found a dollar bill and some loose change. If she needed more money, she'd ask Gilberto for it. She looked at her watch. Time was running out.

She went back to the computer, typed in some more phrases, pulled up some more websites, and submitted her final print requests.

The librarian was waiting when Angela returned from the printer. "Did you find what you needed?" she asked.

"I hope so," replied Angela. "If not, I guess I'll have to come back." Angela shuffled all her papers together. "How much do I owe for the paper?"

"Oh, nothing, dear," declared the woman. "It's just one of our free services. You do have a library card, don't you?"

Angela wondered if those free services were only for library cardholders. "Ah . . . no. Do I need one?"

"We like everyone to have one," said the woman. "It helps us keep track of how many people use the facilities, which helps us get funding. Couldn't run this place without funding. I can get you signed up right now, or we can do it the next time you come in."

Angela looked out the glass doors and saw Steve's truck parked in front of the library. "I really don't have time today," she apologized. "Can I come back next week?"

"Of course, dear," replied the woman. "And bring your friends, especially that preacher man. He's so handsome it does my heart good just to look at him."

Angela grinned and thanked the woman. She thought about hugging her but restrained herself. She'd been doing a lot of that lately. Sure, she was always hugging Steve and Monica, and of course Gilberto, but over the past few months she had also hugged a candy striper, a doctor, the kid at the grocery store, and a costume-loving Cajun. She even hugged her goats. She wondered if all that hugging had anything to do with finally finding love and happiness. No . . . it was probably just all the wonderful people she'd met lately. They were so . . . huggable.

The sky had turned steel-gray and large fluffy snowflakes kissed Angela's face as she left the library. Sticking the papers beneath her jacket, she raced for the truck, and sensing that Monica wasn't about to surrender her prized sentry position, she shook the snowflakes from her hair and slid into the back seat next to Gilberto.

"Did you find what you needed?" he asked.

"Yes," she replied proudly, "and then some." Pulling the stack of papers from

129

beneath her coat, she showed them to Gilberto.

Monica craned her neck and peered into the back seat. "Wow. That's gonna keep you busy for a while."

"I know," mumbled Angela.

After stopping at the local drive-through for cheeseburgers and fries, the four friends headed home. It was already well past two, and they needed to hurry so Angela and Monica could do the afternoon milking before it got dark. The snow that started at the library had continued, and the roads had iced up enough that it was dangerous to drive the posted speed limit. When they finally reached the farm, they were surprised to discover J.B. Walton's Jeep parked in the driveway.

Steve parked his truck next to J.B.'s Jeep and everyone got out. "What's J.B. doing here?" asked Monica as she looked inside the Jeep. "And where is he?"

Angela spotted a light in the milking shed. "Was that on when we left?" She pointed toward the shed.

"I don't think so," replied Monica.

Fearing that J.B. might be up to no-good, the two women raced for the shed.

Monica arrived first, yanked open the door and screamed in horror. "What are you doing to that goat?"

J.B. sat at the milking stanchion with his head pressed into the goat's side and a bucket at his knees. "Milking it," he muttered. "What does it look like?"

"Why?" asked Angela.

J.B. squeezed out a last few drops of milk, covered the pail with a towel, and turned toward Monica and Angela. "I seen all'a'ya leave this mornin' and when I did'n see ya come back, I figured you got stuck in town. Knew the goats would be hurtin' if'n they weren't milked on time so I come up here to take care'a them."

"Where did you learn to milk goats?" asked Monica.

"4-H when I was a kid."

"Well, gee," stammered Monica, "I'm sorry we yelled at you. It's just that we didn't know what was going on. Thank you so much for doing that."

"Tweren't nothin'," replied J.B. "We neighbors gotta watch out fer one another."

This time, Angela didn't hold back. Wrapping her arms around J.B.'s shoulders, she hugged until he pulled away.

"Guess I better get home," he muttered. "The wife'll be wonderin' where I got to." He handed the bucket to Monica, pulled a bandana from his coat pocket, and rubbed his nose briskly.

As he turned to leave the shed, Angela stopped him. "I hope I didn't embarrass you," she said. "Guess I got carried away or something."

"Don't worry about it, ma'am. It were kinda nice."

J.B. lowered his head as he left the milking shed. Even so, Angela noticed something on his cheek. *Was that a tear?*

CHAPTER 9
'TIS THE SEASON

Angela and Gilberto walked arm and arm through the picked-over Christmas tree display at the Family Bargain store. They had sent their gifts and cards out the previous week, but still had to find a tree. So far they'd been to the co-op and K-Mart and found nothing. This place was their last resort.

"I don't know," sighed Angela. "They all look so phony."

Gilberto nodded. "And rightly so. That is why they are called artificial trees. Would you prefer a real tree?"

"Yes," replied Angela, "but I'd feel bad about cutting down a living tree. Besides, our house is so old, a real one might be a fire hazard."

"Maybe we could decorate one of the trees in the front yard."

Angela wrapped her husband in a bear

hug. "See, that's why I love you. You're so smart."

Gilberto grinned and held Angela at arm's length. "And all this time I thought it was because of my charm and good looks."

"Well, that too." Freeing herself from Gilberto's hold, Angela turned and walked toward the front of the store. "Now . . . what about ornaments?"

Thirty minutes later, Angela and Gilberto left the store with a ball of twine, a tube of industrial-strength glue, six boxes of metal ornament hooks, several bottles of gold and silver hobby paint, a pound of corn for popping, and two jumbo packages of brightly colored construction paper.

"What are you planning to do with all that paper?" asked Gilberto.

"Wait and see," chuckled Angela. "Wait and see."

Long before reaching the road leading to the top of the ridge and their home, Angela asked Gilberto to stop the truck at the bottom of a steep hill. Grabbing several sheets of construction paper, she jumped out and asked him to wait.

"Where are you going?" he asked.

"I'll be back in a flash." She slammed the truck door and raced up the steep hill toward little Florence's house.

Florence's mother was standing in the doorway when Angela reached the top of the hill. A diapered infant was in her arms and a dirty-faced toddler peeked from behind her legs. "Heared ya comin'," mumbled the woman. "Lookin' fer Florence?"

"Yes, is she home?" Angela looked beyond the woman into what, in other homes, would have been the living room. Six blanket-shrouded cots lined the walls. There were no rugs on the floor or pictures on the walls. Yellowed rollup shades covered the two windows. A single bare light bulb hung from the ceiling and a towel-covered bucket sat in one corner. Out back, a wood-burning stove, a milk bucket and a butter churn filled up what appeared to be the only other room.

"Nope," replied the woman. "But I'd be obliged if'n you'd come in fer some coffee."

Angela thanked the woman and apologized that she couldn't stay because Gilberto was waiting in the truck. "Maybe some other time? I just dropped by to leave this for Florence." She handed the woman the paper, hugged her and the children, and left. After getting back into the truck, she instructed Gilberto to stop at several more homes. When all the paper was gone, she smiled contentedly and announced, "Okay. Now we can go home."

When they reached their house, Angela and Gilberto were surprised to find Gizmo guarding a very large box on the front porch.

"What's that?" asked Angela.

"I do not know," replied Gilberto. "Maybe the UPS man left it."

"No way," giggled Angela. "You know Gizmo won't let him near the house." Pushing the dog aside, she hurriedly inspected the box. "It's from Katherine and Mongo. What do you think it is?"

"Probably a Christmas present," replied Gilberto.

"All the way from Cuba?" Checking the address label, Angela noticed the box had been shipped from Florida. Before she could investigate any further, the phone rang three times. "Oops, that's our ring." Rushing into the house, she threw her coat on a kitchen chair and grabbed the phone.

"Hi, Angela." It was Pam Walton, their closest neighbor. "The UPS driver dropped a box off here because he was afraid to go up to your place. Said something about a vicious dog chasing him off the place last time he was up there. He wasn't talking about Gizmo, was he?"

Angela laughed. "I'm afraid so. You know

how mean that dog can be."

Pam laughed. "Yes, I do. The first time I met him, I thought he was going to rip my arm right outta its socket. All he wanted was to be petted."

"Yeah, he's kind of insistent about petting."

"Anyway, I sent the boys up with the box. Did you find it okay?"

"Yes, Gizmo the Barbarian took good care of it. Thank the boys for me."

"I will," replied Pam. "Hey, I just put a batch of brownies in the oven. If I can keep them away from the boys long enough, maybe we could share a couple over a cup of coffee later."

"I'd love to," said Angela, "but Gil and I are going hunting for Christmas decorations this afternoon."

"Really? Where?"

"The woods between our place and Steve's. Last time I was down there, I noticed a lot of pinecones and seedpods lying around. If we're lucky, we might even find some nuts."

"Aaah . . . you're doing the whole natural Christmas thing."

"Yes. We decided to decorate that beautiful big evergreen in front of our house, and it just doesn't seem right to put store-bought ornaments on it."

"Well, good luck with that," said Pam. "And let me know if you change your mind about the brownies. I put triple the chocolate in them this time."

"Hmm, don't tempt me."

Completely forgetting about the box, Angela started digging through drawers and cabinets looking for something to hold all the goodies she hoped to find. Discovering a cache of plastic bags, she grabbed a fistful and held them up for Gilberto's approval. "Think this will be enough?"

Gilberto, still wearing his jacket, grabbed a second handful and stuck them into his pocket. "Just in case," he cautioned.

The woods below the ridge were filled with oaks, poplars, redbuds, dogwoods, pines, and a few tenacious black walnuts. The first time Angela had been there was in June when the goats got loose and Gizmo chased after them. Everything was so different back then. The weather was warmer, a carpet of tiny flowers and green vines covered the ground, and all the trees had leaves. Now the flowers and vines were gone, a thin dusting of snow covered the ground, and the trees looked like worn out Civil War soldiers wordlessly waiting for spring to arrive. Angela wondered what kind of soldiers they might have been . . . Confederate or Union? She'd have to ask Gelah.

Gilberto was the first to find anything. "Look, Angela, acorns."

Sure enough, there beneath a tree was a small pile of acorns. But something didn't look right. Didn't acorns fall in a scattered pattern? "I think something or someone else has been collecting these," declared Angela. "Maybe we should leave them alone and find our own." Scanning the area, she spotted more acorns, several black walnuts, and enough pinecones to keep a family of squirrels happy for a month. She quickly filled her bags and half of those Gilberto had brought. Then, noticing that some of the pine trees looked exceptionally full, she brushed the snow away and clipped a few branches. "Cutting one or two branches shouldn't hurt the tree, and I can use them to make wreaths."

Gilberto smiled. "Certo, Angela, certo."

Back at the house Angela sorted through her treasures. With only three days until Christmas, she would have to hurry to get the tree decorated in time for the Christ Child's birth. Sitting at the kitchen table, she painted acorns and attached ornament hooks to pinecones while Gilberto popped and began stringing the popcorn. Stopping only long enough for a quick dinner, they worked until midnight. When the last of the acorns was painted and all the popcorn was strung, Angela made an executive decision. "Let's get some sleep. We've got a busy day ahead of us tomorrow."

The minute her head hit the pillow, Angela drifted toward sleep. In those brief moments before deep sleep took control, she saw herself flying high above the woods. Down below the trees were in full leaf and vibrantly colored birds flitted from branch to branch, catching bugs and singing songs. Her grandson Dominick leaned lazily against a tree. Gizmo was at his side, but the wheelchair was nowhere in sight. The boy waved up at Angela and did a quick two-step. "See, Grams? Now I'm just like all the other kids." Angela's eyes fluttered and the dream disappeared, but the smile on her face lingered until morning.

Gilberto was in the kitchen when Angela finally made her way down the stairs. "Hmm, what smells so good?" she asked.

"French toast," he replied. "I thought you could use a hearty breakfast before starting on the tree. Have you looked outside yet?"

"No. The upstairs windows were frosted over." Heat from the stove had melted the frost from the kitchen window and Angela had to use a dishtowel to wipe away the remaining moisture. "Good grief. There must be two feet of snow out there."

Gilberto shook his head. "The man on the radio said it was three feet. Some of the roads are shut down, and the authorities are warning everyone to stay in their homes because we might get another three or four inches."

Angela's eyes twinkled with pleasure. "That's so exciting," she shouted. "Let's go out and build a snowman or make snow angels. Or how about sledding? We could use some of those moving boxes we stashed in the barn or even old garbage can lids. We couldn't go through the woods, of course, but that sloped area down by the river would be perfect. Oooh . . . what if we get snowed in? Wouldn't that be fun?"

"Calm down, Angela. You are acting as if you have never seen snow before."

"I know," she whined. "But look how beautiful it is. I just wanna go out and play."

"After breakfast," insisted Gilberto.

Angela pretended to pout. "Okay," she mumbled. "But can't we just take a quick peek?"

Reluctantly agreeing, Gilberto walked with Angela to the front door. Angela impatiently yanked open the door and gasped at the solid wall of snow that filled the entryway. "Uh-oh," she groaned. "Looks like we're gonna have to shovel before we play."

Gilberto laughed. "Yes, I believe you are correct. All the more reason to eat breakfast . . . you will need much energy if you are going to shovel all that snow."

"Me?" shrieked Angela. "You mean you're not going to help?"

Gilberto placed a hand on the small of his back and leaned forward. "I am an old man, amore. Do you not remember?"

Before Angela could argue the point, the phone rang. "Are you guys okay up there?" inquired Steve.

"Yes," replied Angela. "Gil and I were just discussing who was going to get the honor of shoveling all the beautiful snow off our front porch."

"Did you get a lot?"

"It's hard to tell. We can't get out the front door to look."

"Really?" chuckled Steve. "Want me to come up and dig you out?"

"No, we should be okay. But if you don't hear from us by noon, send the Mounties up after us."

"I'm afraid all the Mounties are in Canada, Angela. Besides, from what I hear, the hardtop is shut down so they wouldn't be able to reach you unless they rode in on reindeer."

"Wow. What if there's an emergency or something?"

"That's one of the joys of living in the hollows," said Steve. "We're on our own out here and have to take what comes. By the way, don't be too surprised if the phone and electricity go out. Sometimes the utility lines get coated with ice and break."

"What will we do if that happens?"

"Build a fire and send up smoke signals," joked Steve. "Seriously, if the power does go out, you and Gil should come down here. We have a generator and lots of firewood for the stove. You can even bring Gizmo . . . the more body heat, the better."

"What about Christmas?" asked Angela. "If the snow keeps up will you still be able to hold a service?"

"Guess we'll have to wait and see what happens," said Steve. "It's all in God's hands now."

Instead of the predicted three or four, another twelve inches of snow fell, forcing Gilberto and Angela to spend most of the day shoveling. Every time they cleared a path, it quickly filled with more snow. Luckily they lost neither the phone nor the electricity. Late in the afternoon they heard the sound of sleigh bells coming up the ridge.

Gilberto leaned against his shovel. "What do you think that is?"

"I don't know," replied Angela. "It almost sounds like Santa Claus."

The sound grew louder, and before long a hay wagon drawn by two large brown horses pulled into view. J.B. Walton held the reins, his wife, Pam, sat beside him, and their two sons rode in the back. "Brot'cha some cookies," shouted J.B. "Wanted to wait till Christmas, but what with all this snow, Pam were afraid we might not be able to get up here. I bard the horses from old man Cottrell down the road. Tole 'em I'd have 'em back a'fore dark, but if'n we get stuck, we just might haf'ta stay the night."

Angela smiled and offered her hand to Pam. "Were you able to save any of those brownies?"

Pam shook her head. "Of course not. Guess you'll just have to settle for ginger snaps."

"Oh, yum. I haven't had ginger snaps in years," said Angela. "Come on inside, I'll put on a fresh pot of coffee."

The two women busied themselves in the kitchen while Gilberto, J.B., and the boys built a fire in the living room fireplace. Pushing aside some of the Christmas decorations, Pam placed the cookies in the middle of the table. "Looks like a lot of ornaments," she said. "When are you gonna put 'em on the tree?"

"I was going to do it today," replied Angela. "But that was before the snow started. Hopefully the weather will be better tomorrow. If not, I might not get them up in time for Christmas."

Before Pam could say anything else, one of her sons ran into the kitchen. "Quick, I need a broom."

Angela grabbed the kitchen broom from the corner and handed it to the boy. "What's going on?" she asked.

"Sump'ins stuck in the chimney and smoke's backin' up inta the room." Running back into the living room, the boy handed the broom to his father.

Obviously familiar with fireplaces, J.B. threw his coat over the burning logs, leaned into the fireplace and forced the broom, handle first, into the chimney. Almost immediately, small twigs and pieces of broken eggshell fell from the brick-enclosed shaft. "When was the last time ya built a fire?" he asked.

"Not since spring," replied Gilberto. "Up

until lately, it has been too warm."

"Well, looks like a swift done built a nest up there over the summer. Lucky thing them birds don't winter in these parts, otherwise we'd be havin' roasted bird right now."

When Angela started opening windows to let out the smoke, she noticed it had stopped snowing. "Hey, everyone, the snow stopped and the stars are out. Looks like it's going to be a beautiful day tomorrow. Maybe I'll be able to get the tree decorated after all."

"Why wait until tomorrow," asked Pam. "We can do it tonight."

"But it's dark out," objected Angela.

"The boys can build a bonfire, and J.B. can back the wagon up to the tree," said Pam. "That way we won't have to use a ladder to get to the top branches. And . . . if you've got any hot dogs, we could have ourselves an old-fashioned weenie roast."

"Sounds like fun. Let's do it."

Angela and Pam gathered all the tree decorations, pulled two packages of hot dogs, a jar of mustard and some pickles from the refrigerator and headed outside where Gilberto was already directing J.B. to back up toward the soon-to-be-decorated pine tree. A short distance from the tree, far enough away to be safe but close enough to light up the area, J.B. and Pam's sons were stacking logs, teepee fashion, over a large pile of wood chips and wadded up newspaper.

"Don't build that thing so high it sets this whole ridge on fire," cautioned Pam.

"We won't, Maw," replied the boys in unison.

Angela and Pam began hanging the homemade ornaments on the lower branches of the tree while Gilberto and J.B. tackled the upper ones. Within fifteen minutes, all of the ornaments were all in place.

"Looks kinda empty," remarked J.B.

"We still have to put up the popcorn," said Angela. "Anyone have any ideas how to do that?"

"Sure," barked Pam's oldest son. "I'll use my bow." The boy tied one end of the garland to an arrow, placed his feet shoulder-length apart, pointed the bow toward the sky and shot the arrow over the top of the tree. For a moment, it looked as if the arrow was going to take off into outer space, then, just as it cleared the top of the tree, it started downward back toward the earth. With it came the garland. "Now all's we got to do is wrap it around," said the boy.

"Well, I'll be," muttered Angela. "I would

never have thought of that."

"He's a smart one," bragged J.B. "Learned everything he knows from me. Now, did someone say sumpin' 'bout food?"

While Angela handed out hot dogs, Pam began singing. "O Christmas Tree, O Christmas Tree, thy leaves are so unchanging."

J.B. joined his wife. "O Christmas Tree, O Christmas Tree, thy leaves are so unchanging."

By the third line, everyone was singing. "Not only green when summer's here, but also when 'tis cold and drear. O Christmas Tree, O Christmas Tree, thy leaves are so unchanging!"

Like bonfire smoke, the song drifted across the ridge. Down below, the river gently rippled. Somewhere in the distance, a dog barked. And overhead, a star shone brightly.

CHAPTER 10
CHRISTMAS ON THE RIDGE

Christmas dawned bright and cold. It had snowed the night before, but hopefully not enough to keep anyone away from the morning church service. From what Steve had told Angela and Gilberto, it was going to be a simple, down-home celebration with lots of singing and no preaching.

"Don't want anyone falling asleep in the pews," Steve had said.

Angela had volunteered to host a brunch afterwards. "You can do Easter," she'd told Monica, "let me do Christmas." After much debate, Monica had reluctantly agreed, but insisted on helping out. "Thanks," replied Angela, "But I'd sort of like to do this myself."

Now, looking around the kitchen, she wondered if that had been a wise decision. Even though each of the families attending the brunch was going to bring a dish to share, Angela had taken on the responsibility of providing muffins, a fruit salad, and all the beverages. At the last moment, she'd even agreed to bake an old-fashioned country ham. She'd been cooking since four a.m., and now dirty baking pans, mixing bowls and numerous utensils had taken over her kitchen. The service was scheduled to begin in ninety minutes. How could she clean up the kitchen, set the table and get herself ready in that short a time?

As usual, Gilberto came to his wife's rescue. Gently removing her apron, he slipped it over his charcoal-gray suit. "Go upstairs and get dressed, amore. I will take care of the kitchen and set the table."

Angela kissed Gilberto's cheek and straightened his maroon-colored tie. "I love you so much," she whispered.

"I know," he replied. "Now hurry up and get ready. You do not want to be late."

Angela raced up the stairs, clipped her ponytail to the top of her head, took a quick shower, and then slipped into the moss-green velvet dress she'd selected for the day.

Although several years old, the dress had always been one of her favorites. With its fitted sleeves and gathered waistline, it reminded her of Scarlett O'Hara's drapery dress. Of course Angela had never worn her dress to a prison, but her husband was every bit as good looking as Rhett Butler . . . if not more so.

Staring at her reflection in the bedroom mirror, she dabbed on some powder and applied a thin coating of tinted lip-gloss. Next she loosened her hair and let it fall to her shoulders. She didn't normally wear her hair down, but this was Christmas and she wanted to look pretty for the Christ Child. With the aid of a curling iron, she created several long curls, swept them to one side, and secured them with a golden barrette. She was ready.

Gilberto had finished in the kitchen and stood watching as Angela descended the stairs. "Magnifico," he murmured.

Angela extended her hand toward her husband. This was their second Christmas together as husband and wife, and she'd learned a special greeting. "Buon Natale, Gilberto."

"Buon Natale, Angela." Ever so courteously, he bent forward and kissed her hand.

Before heading down the hill to J.B.'s barn-turned-church, Gilberto stopped the truck at the old cemetery adjoining their property. Because of the snow, Angela was wearing boots. But, when she got out of the truck and landed in a snowdrift, the boots quickly filled with snow. Dancing around like one of the Sugarplum Fairies, she cried out, "Brrr, that's cold."

Rushing to her side, Gilberto attempted to pick her up, but she refused. "I'll be all right," she giggled, "but if you wouldn't mind, could you get those wreaths from behind the seat?"

Gilberto retrieved the wreaths and handed them to Angela, who stomped through the snow toward the cemetery. Every step forced more snow into her boots, but she kept going until she reached the entrance gate. She hung one wreath on the gate and continued inside toward a small, weathered tombstone. Brushing away the snow, she revealed the names *Jake and Bertha Withers.*

"Katherine and I found this grave a couple of months ago while she was here," she told Gilberto. "Jake and Bertha were the original owners of Steve and Monica's farm. They had a pretty rough life, but they stayed together . . . even to death." Angela placed the second wreath at the foot of the tombstone and stood back.

"Should we say a prayer?" asked Gilberto.

"No," replied Angela. "I'm sure they're already in Heaven. I just wanted to wish them a Merry Christmas and let them know they were not forgotten."

Gilberto and Angela gazed silently at the

grave for a moment, then Gilberto squeezed his wife's hand. "We can come back later," he said, "right now I am afraid we must leave."

Angela agreed and walked with him back to the truck. When they reached the barn, they were surprised to see all the trucks parked in J.B.'s barren cornfield. One, of course, belonged to J.B. and Pam, another to Sharon and her husband, and two or three to other neighbors. But who owned the other six or seven? And what about the one with Kentucky license plates?

Inside the barn-turned-church, several people sat on metal folding chairs, while a group of twenty-five or thirty stood huddled near the front. Steve noticed Angela and Gilberto enter and waved for them to join him. "Isn't this beautiful?" Sounding very much like a young boy who had just received his very first bicycle, Steve pointed to a large wooden nativity scene filled with two-foot-tall wooden statues: one of Mary with the Child, another of Joseph, and the third of a shepherd grasping a large cane. "J.B.'s cousin, Jethro, carved the statues and built the crèche. When he heard about the fire and what had happened, he decided to bring everything up here all the way from Kentucky."

"T'weren't no big deal," muttered Jethro. "Was comin' up ta see my cousins anyways."

Angela pushed her way through the crowd to get a better look at the wooden figures. Joseph stood slightly behind Mary with his hand placed protectively on her shoulder. Bearing a Mona-Lisa-like smile, Mary held the newborn Child in her arms. The shepherd, who kneeled at Mary's feet, gazed up at her in adoration. Angela sighed and reached out to touch the Child but cautiously pulled her hand back. "He looks so real."

Steve signaled to one of the children in the crowd. The child ran to the front of the barn, picked up a fiddle and began playing. The sound he created was clear and mellow. As people recognized the tune, they began singing. "Silent night, Holy night . . ."

When the hymn was finished, Steve approached the *preacher's perch,* opened his Bible, and asked everyone to be seated. Then he lowered his head and began to read, "This is how the birth of Jesus Christ came to be. His mother, Mary, was pledged to marry Joseph, but before they came together, she was found to be with child. Because Joseph was a righteous man and did not want to expose Mary to disgrace, he had in mind to quietly leave her. But after he had considered this for a while, an angel of the Lord appeared to him in a dream and said, 'Joseph son of David, do not be afraid to take Mary as your wife, because what is conceived in her womb is from the Holy Spirit. She will give birth to a son, and you are to give Him the name Jesus, because He will save His people from their sins.' "

After reading the rest of the story Steve closed the Bible, but true to his word, did not preach. Instead, he raised his hands and began singing. "Oh, Little Town of Bethlehem, how still we see thee lie. Above thy deep and dreamless sleep, the silent stars go by . . ." Stepping down from the makeshift pulpit, he continued singing and motioned for the congregation to join him around the crèche.

The group sang three more songs before Steve clapped his hands together. "I don't know about anyone else," he exclaimed, "but all that singing has made me very hungry. How about everyone following me up to Hummingbird Ridge? Our friends, Angela and Gilberto, have prepared a wonderful Christmas brunch, and we're all invited."

A loud cheer went up as people started

filing out of the barn and jumping into their trucks. Blowing horns and waving out open windows, the parishioners paraded up the road toward the turn off to Hummingbird Ridge. When they reached Angela and Gilberto's house, they waited patiently in their trucks for the preacher and their hosts to arrive.

Gilberto parked his truck alongside the house and summoned everyone to come in. "Per favore di entrare."

Two men climbing out of a truck looked at each other and shrugged. "What'd he say?" asked the first man.

The second man shook his head. "Don' know. Let's just git inside a'fore all the food's gone."

Even though it didn't look as if the little house would hold so many people, it did. Once they filled their plates with green beans, scalloped potatoes, ham, and fruit salad, everyone found a place to sit in the cramped kitchen, the living room, on the stairs, or out on the front porch. Looking every bit like hired security, Gizmo sat at the top of the stairs. No one attempted to dislodge him.

Little Florence and two of her friends approached Angela. "We done whatcha asked, Miz Angela. Now what?" They showed

Angela what they had made with the construction paper.

"Oh, those are so beautiful," exclaimed Angela. "Can you hold on to them until after we're finished eating?"

The girls nodded and scampered away.

Because people had been walking freely in and out of the house, Angela was surprised when she suddenly heard a knock at the door. Not knowing what to think, she walked to the door and opened it. There stood Gelah holding a small wrapped Christmas present.

"My neighbor gave me a ride up here," she said. "I wanted to come to Steve's service, but a couple of my kids called and I couldn't get away in time. Do you think the preacher's mad at me?"

Angela opened her arms to the woman. "How could anyone ever be mad at you? Please . . . Come in."

Gelah looked around the living room, but not seeing a tree, placed the package she was carrying on the coffee table next to several others. "You can open that later," she said. "Right now, I need to say hello to Gil and the preacher."

Angela looked around and saw that her house was filled with wonderful, smiling, family and friends. Everyone was hugging and kissing, laughing at humorous stories, and sharing their joy and happiness with each other. There was a time, not too long ago, that the only person she shared her Christmas with was a dog. But while all of her dogs always gave her loyalty and comfort, how could they comprehend the sacredness or mystery of this Holy Day? That took living, breathing human beings like everyone gathered here at her home. Being surrounded by loving friends made her feel loved. The only people missing were Rebecca, Dominick, Katherine, and Mongo. She would try to call them later.

Breaking into her reverie, Gilberto handed Angela a plate of food. "You have been so busy taking care of everything, I was afraid you would forget to eat."

Angela smiled and accepted the plate. "Thank you, darling, that was thoughtful." She popped a strawberry into her mouth. It was sweet and juicy, very unusual for this time of year. "Everything is going well, isn't it?"

"Yes," he replied. "Sharon's husband told me this was the largest Christmas gathering he had seen in the hollow since he was a child."

"Really? Well, it's not over yet." Angela's smile grew into a mischievous grin.

"There is more?"

"We still have to finish the tree."

Gilberto appeared confused. "What do you mean? I thought we did that last night."

"Not quite. As soon as everyone has finished eating, let's get them all outside."

"Why?"

"It's a surprise. You'll see."

When people started preparing to leave, Gilberto stopped them. "Angela has asked that we all assemble outside before you leave."

"What fer?" asked one of the men. "She gonna make us pray some more?"

"I am not sure," replied Gilberto. "I believe she has something special planned."

When everyone was out of the house, Angela instructed them to gather around the Christmas tree in the front yard. J.B.'s youngest son was already hard at work lining children up around the tree, while his older brother tried to steady a stepladder in the snow. When the ladder wobbled erratically, the older boy called out to his brother. "Come hold this thing so's I don't break a leg."

The younger boy obliged.

On Angela's signal, each child walked up to the younger boy and handed him an object that he, in turn, handed to his brother. The older boy then placed each object on the tree. The objects were home-made construction paper ornaments, some in the shape of stars, others looking like giant gingerbread men. Some had little pictures painted on them, others were adorned with glitter, sequins, and feathers. Each ornament carried a message to the Christ Child and each was signed by the child who'd made it. When all of the ornaments were on the tree, the children joined hands and sang, "Happy birthday to you, happy birthday to you, happy birthday dear Jesus, happy birthday to you."

When the crowd began to disperse, Angela squeezed Gelah's hand. "Can you stay for coffee? Gil and I will drive you home afterwards."

"That would be lovely," replied Gelah.

Gelah and Angela walked arm in arm into the house, sat down on the living room couch, and began chatting about the Christmas brunch. A minute or two later, Gilberto stepped into the room. "Would you ladies prefer coffee or hot chocolate?"

Angela rubbed her hands together. "It was a little brisk out there. Could we have hot chocolate . . . and maybe a fire?"

"Of course." Gilberto stepped toward the fireplace, knelt down, laid a generous handful of wood chips in the grate, and arranged three logs, teepee fashion, over the top. After wadding up several pieces of paper, he stuffed them inside the teepee, lit a match, and touched it to the paper. Leaning back, he watched as flames quickly crawled up the logs. When the wood began to pop and crackle, he stood up and faced the women. "Would you like marshmallows in your hot chocolate?"

Angela lowered her head and displayed a pitiful puppy dog expression. "If it wouldn't be too much trouble . . ."

Gilberto nodded, patted the top of his wife's head and turned toward the kitchen.

"What a wonderful husband," said Gelah.

"Yes, I thank God every day for sending him to me." Angela leaned forward, picked up a small package from the coffee table and handed it to Gelah. "I picked this up for you when I was in Alabama."

The package was wrapped in crinkled gold foil and tied with a sea-green ribbon. Gelah held it in her hands and admired it. "The wrapping is so beautiful it's a shame to open it."

"Go ahead," urged Angela.

Gelah untied the ribbon, carefully laid it aside and slowly removed the paper revealing a small velvet box. Inside the box was the fleur-de-lis brooch Angela bought from Jack Renoux's shop in Stapleton. Removing the pin from the box, Gelah held it up and gazed at it.

"I know you don't wear much jewelry," said Angela, "but the man I bought it from told me the three spikes of the fleur-de-lis represent faith, wisdom, and charity. That made me think about you."

Tears welled up in Gelah's eyes as she pinned the brooch to her left shoulder and kissed Angela's cheek. "I will cherish it always." Pulling a handkerchief from the sleeve of her dress, she dabbed at her face. "Now open yours."

Opening Gelah's gift, Angela discovered a book called *Supergranny — 1000 Fun Things to Do with Your Grandchildren.* "Where did you find this?" she squealed.

"One of my friends gave it to me years ago. I thought you might appreciate it."

"I do," replied Angela. "It's wonderful." She hugged Gelah knowing that the older woman had not just given her a gift, she'd given her a part of her life. This was a gift Angela would never forget.

Gilberto entered the room carrying a wooden tray holding three mugs of hot chocolate, a plate of decorated Christmas cookies one of the guests had brought, and a rawhide bone for Gizmo. Setting the tray on the coffee table, he handed each woman a mug and then called for the dog. "Come here, boy. I have a surprise for you."

As if grateful to be relieved of guard duty, Gizmo lumbered down the stairs and bounded into the living room. Eagerly accepting the rawhide bone, he found a spot near the fireplace, circled around three times to be sure no predators were around, and finally settled down to enjoy his Christmas treat.

Around one o'clock, the phone rang. Gilberto answered it but chuckled and held the receiver out toward Angela. "It is for you," he said.

Angela excused herself and walked into the kitchen. "Hello?"

"Hi, Grams," shouted Dominick, "thanks so much for all the racing chair brochures."

"Oh, I'm glad you got them," said Angela. "I mailed them so late I was afraid they wouldn't get there in time. Have you picked out a style you like?"

"Yeah. I kinda like the *Eliminator,* but the *Top Force* is pretty cool, too. Jack Renoux said if I get one, he'll help me train."

"What do you mean *if?*"

"Well, Mom says those chairs are expensive, and I should find out whether or not I like racing before you go and spend so much money."

"Don't worry about the money, Dominick. You're my only grandchild, and I have fifteen years of Christmases to catch up on. Now, put your mother on the phone and go pick out the chair you want."

"Okay, Grams. I love you."

"I love you back, Dominick."

Was this the way Christmas was supposed to be? Sharing songs and laughter with neighbors, gifts with friends, and love with family? Angela was overjoyed she was finally able to experience it.

After taking Gelah home, Gilberto and Angela ate a quick dinner of brunch leftovers, then sat in the middle of the living room and opened each other's presents. Although they had placed a limit on how much to spend, neither was surprised to find that the other had exceeded the set amount. Angela presented Gilberto with an Italian gelato machine, and Gilberto presented Angela with a ring.

"It's a mother's ring," said Gilberto. "The green stone represents Rebecca's birthstone and the ruby-colored one is Dominick's. The stones are not real, of course, but they are pretty, are they not?"

"No," mumbled Angela. "They are beautiful." She wrapped her arms around Gilberto and hugged until he begged for mercy.

"Per favore, amore. Mollare. You have another package to open."

"Really? Which one?"

"The one from Katherine."

"You're right. I'd forgotten. Where is it?"

"In the closet. I thought it better to put it there so that no one would trip over it."

Gilberto retrieved the box and placed it in front of Angela. After cutting through the corrugated shipping container, he pulled out a second box wrapped in festive paper and topped with a sealed card.

Angela shook the box. "Wow. That's heavy. What do you think it is?"

"There is only one way to find out," said Gilberto.

"You're right," replied Angela. "But let's open the card first."

"Certamente." Gilberto opened the card and handed it to Angela.

A strange expression crossed Angela's face as she read the words written inside. "To make your life a little easier. Love ya both, Katherine and Mongo."

Angela set the card aside and ripped the paper from the box. Then she started laughing.

Inside the second box was a stainless steel

pasteurizer. Katherine might have been hundreds of miles away, but at that moment, her love and friendship filled Angela's heart.

CHAPTER 11
NEW LIFE

With the holidays well behind them, Angela and Monica were spending most of their wakeful hours in the goat pen. Both were excited about the prospect of baby goats and neither wanted to miss the births. They gathered together the vaccines, syringes, and worming kits they'd purchased for the does and prepared for a day of what they called *down home doctoring.* Gilberto and Steve offered to help but were immediately rejected.

"This is woman's work," declared Monica. "You two stay here and watch football or something."

Even though the antenna had blown over in a recent storm and the television transmitted nothing but static, the men didn't argue . . . maybe because they knew it would be useless.

Monica packed all the drugs and equipment into a recycled shoebox and turned toward Angela. "Okay, let's do this." She sounded like a drill instructor giving a command to a group of green recruits. Angela dutifully obeyed.

The goats were playing in their exercise yard when Angela and Monica approached. They still had the teeter-totter from last summer, but now they also had an old telephone cable spool that Steve had bartered for at the co-op. Every time one of the animals jumped on the spool, it sounded like thunder.

The weather was finally warming up and patches of green were popping up wherever nanny berries had landed. Probably thinking they were going to be fed, the goats raced for the fence but stopped short of the electric wire. Angela examined the fence and realized the bottom wire was a good ten inches from the ground. "Do you think we should ask the boys to add another wire?"

"What for?" asked Monica.

"To keep the babies in."

Monica shook her head. "From what I've read, the mother goats will teach the babies to stay away from the wire."

"Really?"

"Yup. Guess it's part of their motherly instinct."

Angela nodded. She was beginning to know that feeling. Every time she talked to Rebecca and found out about the latest careless or wild things Dominick was doing, her heart skipped a beat. When his new racing chair had arrived, he'd jumped right on it, and without reading the instruction manual, immediately took off down the farm's entrance road. Of course, not knowing how to stop, he'd been forced to veer off into one of the soybean fields in order to miss an oncoming car. And just the other day, while trying to see how fast he could go, he'd hit a bump, gone flying from the chair, and landed in a compost pile. Luckily, nothing but his pride had been hurt.

Deciding the easiest way to administer the vaccines was by standing the does on the milking stanchion, Angela opened the milking shed door, allowing Monica to step inside and place the shoebox on top of the supply cabinet. As quick as a flash one of the goats, Sophia, bolted through the open door, jumped on the stanchion, and waited. The goat's udder was swollen and her belly looked as if she'd swallowed a beer barrel.

While Monica prepared the first vaccine, Angela opened the metal garbage can where the dairy feed was stored, scooped up some feed, and placed it in the feeding trough underneath the goat's head. They planned to give each female four different vaccinations — one for tetanus, one for pneumonia, one to improve colostrum, and one containing vitamins. Monica would give the first two, Angela the others. After all the vaccinations had been dispensed, the goats would be wormed. That way, if one of them got *the runs,* the mess would be outside the shed, not inside.

The local veterinarian who'd advised the women which vaccines to buy also told them how to use them: "Wash your hands and wear latex gloves. Use an antiseptic on both the syringe and the medication bottle. Insert the syringe needle into the bottle, pull the plunger back slowly, remove the syringe, point the needle in the air, and check for air bubbles. Clean the injection site. Some people use the area between the forelegs, but I use either the hind or neck area. Give the goat a quick punch to deaden the muscle, insert the needle at a 45 degree angle, and pull the plunger back a short way. Check for blood. If you see blood, you've hit a vein and need to try another spot. If you don't see blood, push the plunger in slowly until all the vaccine is gone. Remove the needle by pulling it straight back, then hold a clean cotton ball to the site until the blood clots. When you get ready for the next injection, use a fresh syringe."

Following the vet's instructions, Monica administered the first and second shots. After each, Sophia bleated and stomped her rear leg in protest, but kept right on eating. Next, it was Angela's turn. With Monica playing supervisor over her shoulder, she nervously filled a syringe, took a deep breath, and stuck the needle into the goat's leg. Pulling the plunger back, she noticed a tinge of red, removed the needle and tried another spot. Two minutes later Sophia was released back into the exercise yard and another goat, Marilyn, had taken her place and started to eat. The last to get her shots was Dolly. By that time, Monica and Angela knew exactly what to do and how to do it quickly. The goat seemed pleased, because it scarcely stomped or bleated.

Within an hour's time, all three does had been vaccinated and wormed, and were lounging peacefully in the early spring sun. Congratulating each other on a job well done, Angela and Monica walked back to the house and treated themselves to a cup of coffee. Before long they started hearing the sound of a goat bleating. Not goats — as in two or three — but just one.

Rising from the table, Angela looked out the kitchen window. What she saw terrified her. It was Bucky, standing on top of the telephone cable spool, screaming at the top of his lungs. Down below, all the female goats lay on the ground, prostrate and seemingly lifeless.

Angela grabbed Monica's arm and frantically pulled at it. "Something's wrong with the goats," she shrieked. Without asking for further explanation, Monica followed Angela out the door.

Clearing the distance between the house and goat pen in what seemed like milliseconds, the women threw open the gate and sprinted toward the downed goats. Angela knelt at Sophia's side, while Monica headed for Marilyn and Dolly. Shouting back and forth to each other, they concurred that all three goats had the same symptoms — their tongues were hanging out, they were breathing heavily, and they all had huge lumps on their hind legs.

"What could have caused this?" shouted Angela.

"I'm not sure," replied Monica. "Maybe it had something to do with the vaccinations. Whatever it was, we can't leave these goats out in the open like this. We've got to move them."

"How?" cried Angela. "They must weigh 75 or 80 pounds apiece."

As if responding to their quandary, Steve and Gilberto appeared.

"What's all the shouting about?" asked Steve.

Monica raised her arms in frustration. "Look around. We've got to get these goats moved before all the neighborhood dogs find out they can't defend themselves."

"Where do you want them?" asked Gilberto.

"How about the barn?" suggested Angela. "That way they'll be protected and we can keep a close eye on them."

"Good idea," agreed Monica. "Maybe we can lay them on a tarp and drag them one by one to the barn."

Steve shook his head. "That might hurt the babies. I'll get my truck and we can put them in the back on a blanket or something. The quicker we get them moved, the better."

"You're right," said Monica. "Get the truck."

Once the goats were safely ensconced in the barn, Angela and Monica got to work filling buckets with water and feed, sending Steve and Gilberto to the house for blankets and pillows, and checking the goats to make sure their symptoms didn't worsen. Steve checked in to say he had called the veterinarian. "The vet said you shouldn't have given them all the shots at one time." That didn't help matters any.

As the day wore on, things seemed to get better. Sophia tried, unsuccessfully, to get to her feet, and Dolly accepted food and water from Angela's hand. By evening, it appeared everything was going to be all right. Even so, neither woman wanted to leave the barn.

"We could have killed them," whispered Angela.

"Don't even think that," responded Monica. "Now wrap yourself in a blanket and let's get some sleep. It's gonna be a long night."

Four days later all of the goats had recovered but Marilyn appeared to have difficulty walking. "Do you think her leg is hurting again?" asked Angela.

Monica shook her head. "Look at her tail. It's more raised than normal, and there are sunken spots along her spine. And look at her udder — it's tight and shiny. I think she's going into labor."

"Really? So soon? I didn't think she was due for another week."

"Well, I guess if she's ready, she's ready."

"How soon do you think it'll be?" Angela began pacing like an expectant father.

Marilyn baaed softly and walked away from Monica and Angela. Then, as she pawed the ground, a stream of creamy mucus dribbled down her legs.

"Any time now," chuckled Monica.

Three hours later a liquid-filled bubble protruded from the doe's rear end. The goat lay on the ground, groaned, and pushed, making the bubble disappear. She didn't seem to be in pain, so Angela offered her food, and just like Dolly, she accepted it. For the next ninety minutes, the bubble reappeared, and with the goat's continued groaning and pushing, disappeared again. After every push, Angela offered more food. From the expression in the goat's eyes, she seemed to enjoy the pampering. The last bubble to appear burst. Something was about to happen.

After four-and-a-half hours of lying down, groaning and pushing, Marilyn stood up and bleated loudly. Another bubble appeared, but this time, instead of liquid, it seemed to contain something else — a tiny brown hoof. The goat pushed, and within minutes another hoof appeared . . . then a nose . . . and finally, a head.

Angela squealed. "It's happening, it's happening."

Monica gasped. "It is. Isn't this wonderful? It's the miracle of life."

With one giant push, Marilyn ejected the kid-filled bubble from her body. Almost as soon as it hit the ground, she turned around, licked the baby's head, cleared the mucus away from its nose and mouth, and then cleaned the remains of the bubble from its tiny body. Thirty minutes later the kid stood up, wobbled under its mother's belly, butted its head into her udder, and drank its first meal.

Hugging each other, Angela and Monica had watched the whole scene unfold. As the baby goat drank its mother's milk, they looked at each other and silently mouthed, "Wow."

"What do you think it is?" whispered Monica.

"I don't know," replied Angela. "Let's look."

Almost afraid to touch the young animal, both women got on their hands and knees and twisted their heads until they could see the baby goat's underside. Then, grinning from ear-to-ear they whispered, "It's a girl."

Two days later, they had another girl from Sophia and twins — one girl, one boy — from Dolly.

"I think we should give the twins to Rebecca," suggested Monica over a cup of morning coffee. "That way she'll have one of each and can start a herd, and Bucky won't get mad at us for adding another male to his herd."

"That's a wonderful idea," agreed Angela as she sat down at the kitchen table. "When do you think they'll be ready to travel?"

"I don't know. Maybe a month or two. It's March now. I'd say the middle of May would be a good time."

"I'll call Rebecca tonight and let her know. She's going to be so pleased."

"Not as much as me," said Monica.

"What do you mean?"

"None of this would have happened without you, Angela. You were the one who wanted to get goats in the first place, and you were the one who talked me into helping with them. Until then my life had been one big mess, and I wanted to give up the whole farm idea, but you turned everything around. I know I don't say this often enough, but thank you, Angela."

Monica and Angela reached across the table and hugged each other just as Gilberto and Steve entered the room. "Why is it every time we turn around, you two end up hugging?" asked Steve.

"Maybe we're starved for attention," joked Monica.

Grabbing her in his arms, Steve bent his wife backwards, leaned over and planted a juicy kiss in the middle of her forehead. "How's that for affection?"

Wriggling free, she stood up and ran her sleeve across her damp forehead. "Yuk. That'll teach me to open my big mouth."

Steve leaned forward again and puckered his lips. "I love your mouth. How 'bout a great big kiss?"

"Haven't you got better things to do?" scolded Monica.

"As a matter of fact," replied Steve, "I do. Easter is only two weeks off, and I haven't started work on my sermon yet."

"My father told me the priest at his church in Italy always invited a monk from a neighboring monastery to preach on Easter," said Gilberto. "That way, the parish priest did not have to prepare a sermon and, the congregation was given the benefit of a different point of view. We do not have any monasteries close by, but maybe one of the ministers from town would agree to come out."

"Great idea, Gil, but do you think we could get anyone at this late date?"

A light went off in Angela's head. "Didn't

Gelah once mention that one of her foster kids was studying to become a minister?"

"Yeah," agreed Monica. "I think it was the youngest boy . . . Henry."

"Okay, then," cheered Steve. "I'll give Gelah a call and see what she thinks about the whole idea."

Gelah, of course, was ecstatic and told Steve that Henry had finished his studies and was living in Lost Creek while waiting for his first assignment. "He can come spend the night with me and then drive both of us to church in the morning. Oh . . . he is going to be so pleased."

On Easter morning, Henry Dobbs and his foster mother were chatting with Pam Walton when Steve parked his truck in front of J.B.'s converted barn. The young man, who looked very wet behind the ears, wore a too-large black suit, starched white shirt, black string tie shaped into a bow, and a somber expression. The only thing missing was a black felt hat.

After making all the appropriate introductions, Steve escorted the young preacher into the converted church and sat next to him on the makeshift altar while the parishioners filed in and took their seats. Aside from Steve, Monica, Angela, and Gilberto, the people attending the Easter service included Sharon and Randy Schuster with their girls, Chester and Mildred Childress, Baxter and Priscilla Phillips, several families from the hollow, Gelah and five of her foster children, Pam and her sons, and surprising everybody, J.B. Walton in pressed chinos and an argyle sweater. His hair looked like he'd slicked it down with 50 weight oil.

Steve stepped up to the pulpit, thanked everyone for coming, reminded them about the brunch afterwards, "Monica was up all night cooking," and informed them he would not be preaching that morning.

Muffled protests rumbled through the church.

"Why not?" asked Baxter Phillips. "Ya run outta words?"

"No," replied Steve. "Today we have the honor of welcoming a brand new preacher to our humble church. He is the foster child of Gelah Spears, whom most of you know, and a young man who's destined to do great things in the name of the Lord. Everyone . . . please say *hello* to Preacher Henry Hobbs."

Henry stumbled to the pulpit, thanked Steve, and hung his head. At first it seemed he was trying to collect his thoughts . . . or nerve . . . but then he seemed to go into some sort of trance.

Several people cleared their throats. One woman mumbled loud enough to be heard, "Think he fell asleep?"

After two long minutes of silence, Henry slowly raised his head, scanned the congregation, and in a loud, booming voice, began his sermon. "Jesus Christ died to save us from our sins. He was mocked, brutalized, and hung from a cross. The guards drew lots to see who would win His cloak and then they stuck a sword in His side." The preacher looked around the room. Obviously aware that he had everyone's attention, he crossed his arms over the top of the pulpit, smirked, and in a contemptuous voice, asked, "So what?"

Gasps broke out. A woman in the second row fainted. An indignant man hurriedly ushered his wife and children out the door.

"Jesus wasn't the first, nor the last, to die a horrible death. There have been others . . . many, many others. His death didn't set Him apart in any way other than maybe its drama and gore. What's really incredible is that He didn't stay dead. Three days after His death, He rose from the tomb and walked among the living."

The solemn-faced preacher stopped talking and looked around the converted barn. Narrow shafts of sunlight streaming through the windows highlighted dust motes drifting in the air. A pair of mourning doves cooed in the rafters. Those people who hadn't left appeared shell-shocked.

"And we can, too, friends. We can rise up from death by being born again in the Lord. All we have to do is believe and trust in Him."

For the next hour, Henry Dobbs preached about believing, trusting, the miracle of Easter, and attaining eternal salvation. He ended his sermon with a quote from the Bible. "Therefore we are buried with him by baptism into death that, as Christ was raised up from the dead by the glory of the Father, even so we also should walk in newness of life. Romans, chapter 6, verse 4."

J.B. jumped out of his chair, raised his face and hands toward heaven, and cried out, "Save me Lord, for I am a sinner."

Henry stepped down from the pulpit and embraced J.B. Then, in a loud, clear voice he declared, "Hallelujah. The Lord has indeed risen and today there is new life."

Chapter 12
Aah Spring . . .

Bam . . . Silence . . . Bam . . .

Angela and Gilberto stared at each other over the tops of their coffee mugs. "What is that noise?" asked Gilberto.

"I don't know," replied Angela. "It sounds like it's coming from Steve and Monica's place. Maybe someone is trying to start up Big Bertha."

"Big Bertha? Who is that?"

"It's not a who, silly, it's a what. You remember . . . it's that old oil well on Steve's property. J.B. told us about it the night we met him." Angela sometimes wondered if age was getting the better of her husband. He'd been forgetting things lately. Nothing of importance, really, just little things like where he left his car keys or what day of the week it was. But then, last week she'd spent thirty minutes looking for her yellow gym shoes because she couldn't remember where she'd left them. So maybe it wasn't just

Gilberto, maybe they were *both* getting old. This was the year she would turn 65. Suddenly, the disparity between her age and Gilberto's was shrinking.

As if reading her mind, Gilberto nodded and knit his brow. "Ah, sì sì . . . the well."

Bam . . . Silence . . . Bam . . .

"Let's go see what that is," urged Angela.

Gilberto lowered his mug to the table. "Right now?"

"Sure, why not? We've done all the chores, had breakfast, and listened to the morning farm report. It's a beautiful day . . . the sun is shining, the birds are singing, and the dogwoods are in bloom. We could take Gizmo for a walk down the hill and find out what's making all that racket. Maybe we could even look for some wild ramps along the way. I hear they're sort of legendary in these parts."

Appearing slightly confused, Gilberto nodded again and followed Angela to the door where Gizmo, obviously anticipating what was coming, sat waiting.

Angela had been right — the day *was* beautiful. Although barely 9 a.m., the temperature already topped 70 degrees. The sky was clear and the sun shone brightly, burning off the morning dew and making the forest feel and smell almost tropical.

Their first full winter on Hummingbird Ridge had been cold and snowy. More snow, in fact, than the area had seen in many years. Some people in the hollow said it was because the United States was under an El Niño weather pattern; others insisted the culprit was La Niña. Erring on the side of caution, Angela steered clear of any and all debates about weather. That was a subject she preferred not to tackle. Now it didn't seem to matter. Spring was here, the rains had washed away what little remained of the snow, and the forest was alive with life and color.

Trees that a few months earlier had appeared naked, were now clad in chartreuse-green leaves and burgeoning buds. Low-growing purple-pink redbud bushes peaked out from under taller white-blossomed dogwoods. Scarlet red cardinals and yellow goldfinches flitted through mountain ash, serviceberry trees, and a towering canopy of black walnut and white oak crowns. Beneath the trees, may apples, wild blue phlox, ferns, yellow violets, and jack-in-the-pulpit grew up through a lumpy blanket of fallen branches, lichens, fiddlehead ferns, and morel mushrooms. Two fox pups poked their shiny black noses out of a den, but quickly ducked back in when they spotted

Gizmo. Before long, baby box turtles would be scampering through the underbrush and the curious canine would have something to chase.

Angela savored all the sights, smells, and sounds that enveloped her, and let them seep into her pores. She felt light-headed, energetic, and fully alive. Of all the seasons, she loved spring the most. It was a new beginning, a time to start over, a chance to put things right. If she'd thought about it, she might have realized it was very much like her life — once almost lifeless — but now full of promise and possibilities. At the moment, however, all she could think about was finding ramps.

"I don't understand," she complained, "they should be all over this place. Do you think it's too early for them?"

Gilberto studied the forest floor. "What do they look like?"

"I'm not sure," she said. "I went looking for them a couple of times when I lived in Indiana but never could find any."

"Maybe that was because you did not know what to look for," suggested Gilberto.

"Could be." Continuing down the hill, Angela noticed J.B. was tilling one of his fields. "Hey, there's J.B. I bet he would know."

"I am sure you are right," agreed Gilberto. "We can ask him after we check out that noise at Steve and Monica's."

"Oh, yeah, the noise. I almost forgot."

Steve and Monica were sitting in lawn chairs outside the goat pen when Angela and Gilberto arrived. True to form, Gizmo sprinted back and forth along the fence, but didn't try to jump the line. Whether or not he'd ever experienced the electric wire, it was good to see he was smart enough to stay away from it.

Bam . . . Bam . . . Bam . . .

Looking toward the milking shed, Angela discovered the source of the noise. Starting from the far end of the pen, the baby goats raced across the grass-covered pasture, and lifting all four hooves off the ground, catapulted off the side of the shed. Hitting the ground, they somersaulted over each other and headed back to the starting point.

"Where'd they learn to do that?" laughed Angela.

"I think it comes naturally," chuckled Monica. "They've been doing it all morning."

"We know," replied Angela. "We could hear them all the way up at our place."

"Oh no," groaned Monica. "Do you think everyone in the hollow can hear them?"

Leaning forward in his chair and donning a cherubic smile, Steve volunteered his expert knowledge. "That all depends on how you look at it. You see, the velocity of sound is 1087 times the square of 273 plus temperature, divided by 16.52. If the temperature in the hollow is 72 degrees, then the velocity of sound would be 1218 feet per second. The hollow will echo sound, but the trees weaken the signal as the waves are bounced from tree to tree. Because of the trees, the sound waves will diminish in intensity, but not in velocity."

Gilberto and Monica gawked at each other in bewilderment.

"Well, thank you, Mr. Wizard," cackled Angela. "I didn't know our preacher was such an educated man."

The plastic lawn chair creaked as Steve leaned back and grinned. "Ah shucks," he slurred, "twern't nuttin'."

Everyone laughed so hard that Gizmo abandoned the goats and ran to his mistress' side. Once satisfied she didn't need help, he returned to running the fence.

Steve pointed at two vacant lawn chairs. "Sit down and enjoy the show," he said.

"No, thanks," replied Angela. "We just came down to make sure everything was all right. Now that we know it is, we've got to go down the road and talk to J.B."

"What about?" asked Monica.

"Ramps."

"Why go all the way down there?" inquired Steve. "I've got some in the barn you can borrow."

Angela squinted at Steve then burst out laughing. "Not those kind of ramps . . . the kind you eat."

Steve's expression indicated he had no idea what Angela was talking about.

Linking arms with Gilberto, Angela turned away. "Now *I* know something you don't," she bantered.

J.B. was driving a large-wheel tractor back and forth across the farthest corner of his property. The red paint on the tractor was dulled by years of neglect but the words Massey Ferguson stood out bright and proud. Trailing behind the tractor, a multi-pronged plow tore through the loamy soil, turning over the upper layer and burying what few weeds had managed to take hold.

Gilberto waved his arms high in the air trying to get J.B.'s attention, but it took several minutes before the tractor stopped and J.B. jumped off. Heading toward Gilberto and Angela, he slapped dust and dirt from his faded bib coveralls, pulled a stained bandana from his back pocket and wiped his grimy face and neck. "Well, I'll be a pig in a poke. Ya'll come to help?"

"Well, sure," stammered Angela. "What can we do?"

J.B. laughed so hard a wad of chewing tobacco fell out of his mouth. Kicking it aside, he apologized, "Sorry 'bout that. Plowin's dusty work and the chaw helps some."

"Not a problem," replied Angela. "My dad used to chew."

Gilberto raised a hand to shield his eyes and surveyed the half-plowed field. "What are you going to plant here?"

"Field corn," replied J.B. "Sell most'a it to the co-op but hold back enough fer my livestock and next year's crop."

"Can you make a living from it?" asked Angela.

"Well . . . I us'ly average 100 bushels per acrc and I plant better'n 150 acres. Last 'cher the co-op paid a buck a bushel, so I ended up makin' about fifteen thousand give or take. Soybeans pay two bucks a bushel, but my animals won't eat 'em, so I stick with corn. Sides, I'd hafta buy all sorts of new equipment for soybeans, so I'd prob'ly end up losing money."

Angela wondered if Rebecca was making any profit on her soybean crop. If not, maybe she could plant corn. "My daughter grows soybeans on her farm in Alabama."

J.B. looked stunned. "Didn' know ya had a dautter . . . whats 'er name?"

"Rebecca. She and her son run a migrant worker farm down on Mobile Bay."

"Ya got a gran, too? Well, I'll be." J.B. whipped out his bandana again and wiped sweat from the back of his neck.

"Yes, his name is Dominick. Maybe you'll get to meet him one day." Angela thought about telling J.B. that her grandson was in a wheelchair, but standing out in an open field with the glorious sun baking her winter-white arms didn't seem like either the right time or right place.

Looking eager to get back to work, J.B. stuffed the bandana back into his pocket. "I'd like that," he mumbled. "Now, whatch'all come down here fer?"

"Angela and I want to search for ramps," said Gilberto, "but we do not know what they look like or where they grow. Can you tell us?"

J.B. laughed. "You prob'ly won't find any 'round here fer a nutter week or two. If'n you really want to find some right away, ya gotta head off down the udder side'a the ridge or check out the river bottom. Saw a bunch there las' week."

Angela's face brightened. "Really?"

"Yup. But why in the world are ya lookin' fer 'em? You ain't gonna eat 'em, are ya?"

"That's the plan. I hear they're really good fried in bacon grease and mixed into scrambled eggs."

J.B. chuckled to himself and slid a fresh wad of chewing tobacco into his cheek. "Tell ya what . . . they're holdin' a ramps festival in town this weekend. If you kin wait till tomorrow, I'll buy you a ramps dinner. That way you'll know what they look like and if'n ya think they're even worth huntin' fer."

"That sounds like fun, doesn't it, Gil?"

Gilberto agreed, and before allowing J.B. to return to work, volunteered to drive J.B. and his family to the festival.

"Thanks," declined J.B., "but I think I'd better drive myself. Your truck ain't big enough fer all'a us."

"Really?" questioned Angela. "I thought your kids always rode in the back."

"They do 'cept when it rains, and they're predictin' rain tomorrow, so they'll prob'ly wanna ride inside."

Angela suspected J.B. was making excuses, but she couldn't figure out why. Did he just not want to ride with her and Gilberto or was there some other reason? Rather than pursue the matter, she let it drop. "When

192

and where should we meet?"

"How's twelve o'clock at the high school ball field?"

"Okay . . . we'll see you there."

While milking the goats the following morning, Angela told Monica about her encounter with J.B. "Sometimes I can't figure that man out. First, he invites us to the ramps festival, but when Gil offers to drive, he turns us down flat. It was almost as if he didn't want to be seen with us."

"Maybe he just didn't want to be an imposition. You know how these country people are."

"No. I think it's something else."

"Like what?"

"I don't know, but I'll probably find out when we go to the festival. By the way, we've got room in our truck, wanna come with?"

Monica leaned her head into Dolly's flank. Since producing twins, Dolly had been giving more milk than ever before. The only problem was that she wanted to save it for her babies. Leaning into Dolly's side seemed to calm her, and she always ended up relinquishing her creamy white treasure. "That depends," mumbled Monica. "What's a ramps festival?"

"I'm not really sure," admitted Angela. "I looked up ramps in one of our farm books, and all it said was they are 'a pungent wild leek that tastes like a cross between onions and garlic, and that Appalachian people celebrate spring with its arrival.' Guess they make them into a tonic to ward off winter ailments."

"Hmmm . . ." replied Monica. "Sounds interesting, but let me check with Steve and make sure he doesn't have anything else planned. And maybe we could leave early and stop at the co-op. We need more cheese-cloth and rennet. With all the extra milk we're getting, we've just about run out of both, and I want to make cheese next week."

Clarence Higby was getting ready to close the co-op when Monica and Angela walked through the door the next day. "Y'all better hurry. I'm in charge of the Jumpin' Castle at the festival and got to get over there 'fore the kids tear the whole thing down."

"We just need rennet and cheesecloth," stated Monica.

"Rennet's over there by the canning supplies." Clarence pointed to the far wall. "Outta cheesecloth, but some's due in end'a next week if'n you kin wait that long."

"Guess we'll have to," replied Monica.

Angela was leafing through a cheese-making book when Monica joined her at the canning supplies. "There's a recipe in here for making blue cheese. Wouldn't that be great on fettuccine with a big salad and some of Gil's fresh bread?"

"As much as you like food, you should be as big as a house."

"Jealous?"

Angela spotted a Ball Blue Book next to the enameled water bath pots and started scanning through it. "Ours got splattered last year when the Gizmo Camp kids were helping us can tomatoes."

"Put that down, Angela. I already bought a new one." Monica took the book from Angela's hand and placed it back next to the pots. "Let's just get the rennet and leave so Mr. Higby can close up. Besides, Steve and Gil are probably wondering what's taking us so long."

Angela nodded, then followed Monica to the cash register. Once outside, they rejoined their husbands and headed for the high school.

Looking for but not finding J.B.'s truck, Gilberto parked his truck about four rows back from the entrance. "We are early," he observed. "Shall we look around or wait here until J.B. and his family arrive?"

"Let's look around," suggested Angela. Like the day, her mood was bright and cheerful. The last festival she'd attended had been with Katherine and Mongo. Gil had just returned from Alabama, Katherine had bought a sunbonnet, and she had gotten the news that she didn't have cancer. *Was that just six months ago?* It seemed like a lifetime.

Climbing out of Gil's truck, Monica immediately wrinkled her nose and looked around the parking lot. "What's that horrible smell?"

"I don't know," said Steve. "Is the wind blowing from the stockyards?"

"There is no wind," Monica replied sarcastically. "Besides, I don't think any self-respecting cow could *ever* smell that bad."

"No," added Angela. "It's like really, really bad body odor."

Two teenage girls walked past the truck where the four friends were standing. Monica took a deep whiff as the girls walked by then quickly held her nose. "Good grief, I think that smell is coming from them."

About that time, J.B. drove up, honked his horn, and yelled out the window, "Are ya ready for this?" Surprisingly, J.B.'s sons were not in the truck. Had he already dropped them off or had they simply not come? Something didn't seem right.

Everyone piled into the high school cafeteria where a line of would-be diners were standing in the serving line waiting to be fed — some carried trays, others were empty-handed. Six hair-netted, white-aproned women stood at attention behind the serving counter. The food stations in front of them were empty. A loud cheer broke out when several young boys carried in heavy-looking aluminum trays and placed them in the food stations. The hair-netted ladies dug into the aluminum trays, filled plates, and handed them to the diners who then paid for their meal and quickly found a place to sit.

"You ladies find a table 'fore they all fill up," instructed J.B. "Us men 'ill git the food."

The tables were standard cafeteria fare, about seven feet long with a beige laminated finish emblazoned with the initials of count-less successions of upper and underclass-men. Eight bruised and battered folding chairs flanked each side. A single black nursery pot holding perky golden marigolds was the only table decoration.

Pam suggested a table near the open door, a good choice since the noxious odor expe-rienced in the parking lot seemed even stronger in the enclosed area. A few minutes later, J.B., Gilberto, and Steve, each bearing two plates piled high with cooked ramps, joined their wives.

"Dig in," said J.B.

"Buon appetito," offered Gilberto.

"Yeah. That, too," concurred J.B.

After the meal, J.B. and Pam headed for home, while Steve, Monica, Gilberto, and Angela stuck around the festival and walked off their meal. Steve commented he'd enjoyed the ramps, but Monica said they weren't to her liking. "Maybe if I hadn't eaten so many . . . I don't think I'll be able to taste anything else for at least a week."

As they walked around the numerous souvenir booths, they kept smelling that same strange odor. It wasn't just coming from the teenage girls, it was coming from everywhere. Eventually they became so used to the smell they hardly noticed it. The same, however, was not true the following morning.

Standing outside J.B.'s barn church, Angela noticed several parishioners back away when she said good morning to them. Afraid she might have forgotten to put on deodorant, she sheepishly raised her right elbow and sniffed her underarm. *No, that wasn't the problem.* So, what was?

J.B. walked up, grabbed her by the shoulders, looked straight into her eyes, and huffed the word, *Hi,* in her face.

The stench almost knocked her over. "Good grief, J.B. What have you been eating?"

"Ramps." J.B. grinned and waited for the truth to sink in. It didn't take long.

"Oh, no. Do I smell like that, too?"

"Yup," he replied.

Angela looked as if she wanted to run away and hide. "What can I do about it?"

"Nuttin'. Jist gotta let it work outta your system."

"How long will that take?"

J.B. scratched his chin and tried to look pensive. "A week . . . maybe two."

Angela suddenly realized why J.B. had refused Gilberto's offer to drive to the festival. It wasn't because he didn't want to be seen with them . . . it was because he didn't want to have to ride home with them. Evidently eating ramps wasn't a problem . . . smelling them on someone else was.

Angela promised herself she'd never eat the noxious plants again . . . Now all she had to do was convince Gilberto, Steve, and Monica to promise the same thing.

CHAPTER 13
TRAINING WHEELS

More and more, getting up in the morning was becoming quite an adventure for Angela. Each day was different from the next, and even though there were a few she might not care to repeat, they were all amazing.

Just as she was preparing to head down to the goat pen one Saturday morning, the phone rang. One ring . . . two rings . . . Yes, it was their signal. She removed the receiver from its cradle on the kitchen wall and spoke into the mouthpiece. "Hello?"

"Hi, Mom, it's Rebecca."

Mom? When had Rebecca started calling her Mom? Even though Angela was Rebecca's birth mother, hearing herself being called *Mom* was a bit of a shock. After all, she'd met Rebecca less than five months ago. Did that qualify her to be called a mother?

"Uhh . . . hi, Rebecca. This is a nice surprise. How are you?"

"I'm great," replied Rebecca. "Listen . . . I hope you don't mind me calling you Mom. It's just that Angela sounds so formal, and after all you've done for me and Dominick, I feel like we're family."

"What did I do?" Aside from the few Christmas and Easter gifts she'd sent, Angela had no idea what Rebecca was referring to.

"You've given me back my son," replied Rebecca

Now she *was* confused. Had Rebecca and Dominick been having problems, and if so, what had she done to help resolve them? "What on earth are you talking about, Rebecca?"

"Dominick. In case you didn't notice when you were here, he was acting pretty rebellious. He'd go off and do what he wanted to do, when he wanted to, and with whomever he wanted to do it."

A strange feeling in the pit of her stomach warned Angela to tread lightly. "Really?"

"Yes. When he started high school, he started acting like he knew everything, and then he began hanging around with some pretty unsavory characters."

"You mean like the men down on the bay?" Angela immediately regretted her words. Dominick had cautioned her not to talk about those men, but at the drop of a hat, she'd gone and spilled the beans. So much for earning her grandson's trust.

"How did you know?" Shock and surprise registered in Rebecca's tone.

Angela knew she had to be careful. If she revealed too much, Dominick would get angry, and Rebecca might be resentful if she thought Dominick had been confiding in his grandmother instead of her. "Dominick told me about them," she lied.

There was an uneasy silence on the line.

"When was this?" asked Rebecca suspiciously.

"The day we met at the farm," confessed Angela. "Remember . . . he took me for a ride in his truck."

Another silence.

"What else did you talk about?"

"The usual," replied Angela. "School, girls, his truck . . ."

"What did he say about the men?" Rebecca didn't sound ready to drop the subject.

"Not much. Just that they were shrimpers and moored their boat somewhere down on the bay."

"Did he also tell you they were teaching him to drink?"

Angela was glad she and Rebecca were

having this conversation on the telephone. If they had been face-to-face, Angela wouldn't have been able to conceal her guilt. "No, of course not." She tried to sound convincing. Evidently, it worked.

"I guess he'd been driving his truck off the farm property without me knowing and met those guys when he ran into a ditch one day. They pulled his truck out of the ditch and offered him a drink, which he took, and he started running around with them on a regular basis."

"Do the men work on the farm?" Angela grimaced when she realized her question might indicate she knew the men were immigrants.

"No," replied Rebecca. "I guess they just fish and live on their boats."

"So how did you find out about them?" asked Angela.

"Right after Dominick started training on his racing chair . . . you know he's been training with Jack, don't you?"

"Yes . . ." Angela dragged the word out hoping Rebecca would get on with her story.

"Well, we were at the Piggly Wiggly one day, and these three grubby-looking men walked up to us, and one of them said 'Hey, Jefe, where you bin?' You know . . . just like he was talking to an old friend. Anyway, I thought he might have been talking to someone behind us, so I turned around to look, but no one was there. When I turned back, I saw Dominick trying to wave all three of them away. The guys took the hint and disappeared around the end of the aisle before I could ask them anything."

"What makes you think they'd been drinking together?"

"When we got home I asked Dominick about the incident at the store, and he told me everything."

"Everything?" Did that include her part?

"Yes. Taking the truck, meeting the men, even drinking tequila or whatever it was they were giving him. Why? Do you think there's more?"

"No." Had Dominick picked up the lying gene from her? "Then what happened?"

"Almost overnight, he changed. He started spending a lot of time training with Jack, sometimes they're gone for hours. Also, Dominick got a part-time job to help pay for more equipment, and he promised never to drive off the property without my permission again. If you hadn't sent him that racing chair, none of that would have happened. Would you believe . . . he even found a girlfriend."

"You're kidding."

"I'm not. Her name is Esperanza. That means hope."

"I know," chucked Angela. She was glad the conversation was headed in a new direction. "She and her family live here on the farm, and she rides to school with Dominick every day. From what I hear she's a grade A student. She's such a pretty thing — long black hair, big brown eyes, and a beautiful smile that just melts everyone's heart. She said she'd seen Dominick with Jack and wanted to know what all the training was about. When he told her he was going to race in a marathon, she offered to help."

"That's so sweet," said Angela.

"Yes, but here's the really interesting part. It seems her uncle, who still lives in Mexico, is a wheelchair-racing champion, and he's going to come up for Dominick's first marathon."

"How wonderful," exclaimed Angela. "When is the marathon?"

"May fourteenth," replied Rebecca.

Angela flipped the page of the calendar hanging next to the phone. "That's Mother's Day."

"Yes," agreed Rebecca, "and I was hoping you and I could celebrate together."

Angela quickly considered what might be

happening on the farm in the upcoming weeks. The vegetable garden would be planted by late April, the first haying-cutting probably wouldn't happen until the end of May, and the baby goats would be weaned in the next week or two. There was no reason she couldn't be gone for a couple of days, and she was sure Monica wouldn't mind taking over milking-duty while she was away. "Perfect," she said. "Gil and I could even bring the kids down if you still want them."

"I do," replied Rebecca enthusiastically. "This place is being taken over by kudzu. Will you need any help getting the goats down here?"

"No. Gil's truck has one of those shells over the bed. He said he'd clear everything out, put rubber mats and hay on the floor, and rig up something so the goats would have food and water while we're on the road. There's plenty of ventilation, even a fan in the roof. If we drive straight through, everything should be okay."

"That's an eight-hundred-mile trip," observed Rebecca.

"I know, but we'll take turns driving and we've got lots of John Denver CDs, so it shouldn't be too bad. Will you be able to put us up while we're down there, or should

I make reservations at the Bayview?"

"Dominick has been cleaning up one of the vacant houses. He's been patching, painting, and spit polishing everything in sight. He even dragged me to Mobile to buy new curtains and bed linens. Said he wanted to be sure his Grams had someplace nice to stay whenever she came down."

"Grams?" chuckled Angela. "How'd he come up with that name, anyway?"

"He told me it was the name of the grandmother on the TV show, *Charmed*."

Angela frowned at the phone. "That show was about witches . . . wasn't it?"

Laughing so loudly that Angela had to hold the receiver away from her ear, Rebecca explained that Dominick didn't think his grandmother was a witch. "That was his favorite show growing up. He has the whole series on tape — all 178 episodes."

"Wow. Talk about loyal fans."

"I know," agreed Rebecca. "Sorry, Mom, but the exterminator just pulled up in front of the house. We've got some sort of infestation around the foundation, and I want to make sure that whatever it is doesn't move inside. Oops, he doesn't look too happy. Guess I better run. Can I call you back next week?"

"I'll call you," replied Angela.

"Thanks, Mom, I love you."

"I love you too, Rebecca." Angela blew her daughter a kiss and hung up the phone. Two seconds later, it rang again. Once . . . twice.

Laughing quietly, she grabbed the receiver. "Did you forget something?"

"I don't think so," answered her brother.

"Tony?"

"None other. How ya doin' baby sister?"

"Okay," she replied. "How about you?" Even though Tony had spent sixty days in alcohol rehab, Angela knew he was having trouble controlling temptations and following the Twelve Step Program. Telling him how truly wonderful her life had become would probably just depress him.

"I have good days and bad days," admitted Tony.

"Have you been praying?"

"Yeah, but God doesn't seem to be listening. Either that, or He's ignoring me."

Angela hesitated before commenting. Before meeting Steve and Monica, she'd stayed away from prayer and church long enough to know how difficult it was to return. That first night in Steve's triple-wide trailer in Egret Cove, all she wanted to do was crawl under her chair and hide. But she hadn't. She kept going back to Steve's services time after time, and now God was so much a part of her life she couldn't imagine starting or ending a day without thanking Him for all the marvelous gifts He had given her. She had no idea if anything she might say would make any difference to Tony, but she had to give it a try.

Taking a deep breath, she told him, "Maybe you're not trying hard enough."

"What's that supposed to mean?" barked Tony.

"I don't know. Maybe you've got to keep pounding on Heaven's doors until someone answers. A friend of mine once told me a story about St. Peter and the Pearly Gates. It seems St. Peter was very fussy about who he let into Heaven and who he sent elsewhere. One day he looked around and noticed there were a lot of people standing around who didn't belong there."

"Yeah? Where did they belong? Hell?"

"Yes," she replied confidently.

"Okay, I'll bite. How'd they get into Heaven?"

"God got so fed up with all the people pounding on the front door, that whenever St. Peter turned his back, He snuck them in the back door."

"Hardy, har, har. Tell your friend he needs new material. That one's so old it's got whiskers."

"Seriously, Tony. If you don't think God is listening to you, keep pounding on His door. Sooner or later, He'll answer. You might not get the answer you were looking for, but at least you'll get an answer."

Tony sighed deeply. "When did you go and get so religious?"

"I'm not particularly religious, Tony, I just believe God helps anyone who puts their trust in Him."

"Well that's all fine and well for you, Angela, but I don't believe any of that baloney. We live in a tough world. We're born, we die, and no one helps us along the way except ourselves."

Angela reached to her neck and felt the gold charm hanging there. "Do you remember that charm you gave me on my wedding day?"

"The one of the little girl on a bicycle? What about it?"

"You said you were giving it to me in case I ever needed to find my way back home. But I always thought there was more to it, more than you were saying."

"Like what?" mumbled Tony.

"I always thought it was your way of saying you were always there for me and always would be."

"You're my kid sister. I only did what a big brother was supposed to do."

"No, Tony. You did more. When I got my first bike, Dad wanted to put training wheels on it so I wouldn't break my neck, but you told him I didn't need training wheels. You said you would teach me to ride without them."

"Big deal," muttered Tony. "So I taught you how to ride a bike. What's that got to do with all this stuff about God and praying?"

"Even though I was frightened, I trusted you. Sure, I got my share of bumps and bruises, and there were times I wanted to give up, but you hung in there and taught me how to ride . . . without training wheels. God doesn't use training wheels either, Tony. He just takes people by the hand and guides them through their darkest moments. All they have to do is trust in Him."

"I can't, Angela, and I don't. In fact, I'm not even sure there is a God. Maybe He's just a figment of everyone's imagination. Too many bad things have happened in my life, and if there is a God, He's the one who let them happen. If He is as wonderful as you make Him out to be, why does He let so many bad things happen?"

Angela knew Tony wasn't the first, nor

211

would he be the last, to ask that question. Even she had wondered about it. Why had God allowed her first husband to cheat on her? Why had He put her through the torment of thinking she had cancer, or that her friend, Gelah, was trying to steal Gilberto away? Why did He allow Steve's church to burn down? Why had He given Dominick spina bifida and taken Rebecca's husband in a drive-by shooting? Why did He send tornadoes, earthquakes, hurricanes, and terrorists to kill thousands of innocent people? She didn't know, but she had to say something to Tony to give him hope.

"When something bad happens to me, I try to figure out what God's purpose is in letting it happen. Is He trying to teach me something? Is He testing me? Does He want me to follow a new path? Sometimes I get an answer, sometimes I don't. Either way, I trust that He, above all others, knows *what* He's doing and *why* He's doing it."

"If life were that simple, Angela, there would be a lot more happy people in this world."

Sensing that Tony had raised his armor and wasn't going to listen to any more talk about God, Angela shifted gears. "Oh, talking about happy people — my grandson is going to race in his first marathon on

Mother's Day, and Gilberto and I are going down to watch him."

"I thought he was in a wheelchair."

Angela explained about the racing chair she and Gilberto had given Dominick for Christmas, talked about taking the goats down to Rebecca, and expressed her excitement about celebrating her first-ever Mother's Day. Tony didn't seem interested in anything she said. In fact, after five minutes of listening to his sister's joyful prattle, he cut the conversation short and hung up.

Totally drained by the experience, Angela leaned her forehead against the still-warm telephone and sighed. "Dear God, please help my brother. I pray for him every day and try to talk to him about You, but he doesn't want to listen. How can I get through to him?"

Deciding it was too late to help Monica with the milking, Angela grabbed a light sweater and headed across the ridge toward the cemetery. The sun had already burned off the morning mist allowing the wildflowers and grass to sway in the gentle breeze that smelled of leaf mold. She removed her shoes and socks and let the vegetation tickle her toes. Other people might think of these wild plants as weeds, but she saw them as more examples of God's goodness. Aside from just supplying food and shelter for numerous animals, the wild plants brought color and beauty into the world, making it a friendlier place to be.

Ten feet ahead, a bright red cardinal pecked at a clump of ground ivy. Another of God's wonderful creations, she wondered if the bird was looking for insects or simply admiring the plant's delicate violet-blue blossoms?

Not wishing to disturb the bird, Angela stood still and considered how fortunate she was. In her almost sixty-five years, she'd been through some pretty rough times, but nothing compared with what Tony had experienced. She'd never had to watch over a pesky sister or teach anyone how to ride a bike; she'd never had to join the Army or fight in a war; she'd never had to worry about running a business or raising a family.

What had started Tony drinking in the first place? Was it an illness? Did it have something to do with his childhood? He'd done the right thing by going to rehab, but he had to do more to keep himself from falling back into old habits. In Angela's way of thinking, that meant turning to God.

Simple pleasures like the warmth of the morning sun, the smell of the ancient forests, and the songs of birds in the trees filled Angela with incredible joy. Ever since marrying Gilberto and moving to West Virginia, her life had taken on new meaning. Somehow the sky seemed bluer, the grass greener, the birds more melodious. Seeing with new eyes and hearing with new ears, she felt fully alive. But how could she feel so good when her brother was suffering?

Dropping to her knees, Angela hung her head and wept.

CHAPTER 14
ALL IN A DAY'S WORK

The rebuilding of Steve's church was going better than anyone had expected. During the winter months, the charred remains had been demolished and hauled away, plans had been drawn up by a local contractor, and new lumber and prefabricated roof trusses had been ordered. Now that spring had arrived, construction had begun, and if everything went as planned, the little church would be ready for whatever came its way before summer.

Everyone in the hollow pitched in. Regardless of the weather, J.B. and his sons spent most Saturdays sawing and hammering around the site. Sharon Schuster's daughters, clearly infatuated with J.B.'s sons, made sure the boys always had enough sandwiches and cookies to keep their hunger at bay. Gelah sent her foster children to help and even organized several in-town bake sales to raise money for shingles, flooring, and windows. Mr. and Mrs. Cottrell, from down the road, showed up several times, as did little Florence, her brothers, sisters, parents and most of the other kids from Camp Gizmo. Even the contractor and his crew, who volunteered their time and services, had made regular appearances.

Truckloads of recycled and overrun lumber had begun arriving at the construction site in late February. By mid-March, the windows and shingles sat stacked up next to the lumber, and during a warm spell in April, new subflooring had been put down over the somewhat scorched but still functional stone foundation. Once the walls were in place, the roof would go up and then work could begin on the interior. Getting those walls up, however, might be a problem. After all, it had once taken Angela's ex-husband two months to erect the prefabricated walls of an eight by ten aluminum garden shed. How long might it take to get the walls of a church built and put up?

When Angela told her daughter what was going on at the church, Rebecca suggested the quickest way to get the walls up might be by holding an old-fashioned barn raising. "We had one down here when we were building our church. The whole community worked on it, including a lot of people from town. The men did the building, the women provided the food, and the kids acted as go-fers."

Angela shook her head. "You mean those little furry animals that tear up people's lawns?"

"No, Mom," giggled Rebecca. "Gofers fetch things. You know . . . they *Go* for things. The kids carried supplies, tools and water to the men so they wouldn't have to get down off their ladders or stop working whenever they needed something."

"Sounds like everything was well-planned," remarked Angela. "Do you think a barn raising would work up here?"

"I don't see why not," said Rebecca. "All it takes is a little planning."

After listening to her daughter report the latest news from Mariposa Landing, "The peach trees are in bloom, Dominick is up to twenty miles a day in his racing chair, and his girlfriend invited him to the Spring Fling at school," Angela hung up the phone and got to work.

Grabbing a yellow legal pad and ballpoint pen, she jotted down some ideas — call the neighbors, put up flyers at the grocery store and co-op, create work lists, and check sup-plies. As an afterthought, she added — order T-shirts and come up with a grocery list for a barbecue. Just because this was a work project, it didn't have to be *all work.*

Three weeks later, fifty workers of every shape and size swarmed around the soon-to-be-restored church. Wearing canary yellow T-shirts with the words "God is Great" emblazoned across their chests, they made quick work of the five gallons of coffee and eight dozen chocolate donuts Jasper, the grocery clerk, had generously provided.

Shielding her eyes from the intense morning sun, Angela surveyed the work scene. Several women were using gas-powered circular saws to cut 20-foot lengths of lumber into shorter lengths while two teams of men — one made up of J.B. and his sons, the other of Gilberto, Steve and one of Gelah's foster children — set the cut pieces on the church subfloor and hammered them together to form a rectangular box. Sharon meticulously checked the corners of each box with a metal t-square and Pam followed behind with a level. The idea was to assemble two 36-by-12-foot walls and two 20-by-12-foot walls on the subfloor, make sure they were square, apply sheathing, then raise and nail them in place. Although it all sounded fairly simple, the sweat on Gilberto's brow was an indication that this was not going to be an easy task.

Angela called little Florence over and handed her six icy bottles of spring water. "Take these to the men working on the walls," she instructed, "especially the white-haired one."

Florence nodded and skipped away. When she delivered one of the bottles to Gilberto, he turned around and blew his wife a kiss. It was just one of the many things he did each day that made Angela's life a joy.

In the distance, the annoying sound of grinding gears reverberating through the hollow caught everyone's attention. J.B.'s sons and several other teenage boys abandoned their work posts and ran down the hill to see what was happening. As the noise grew louder, a large yellow truck came into view. Behind the truck was a long-bed trailer and mounted on the trailer was a crane.

Blocking all traffic, the truck and trailer came to a stop on the road just below the church. A portly man about the same age as Gilberto, maybe a bit older, jumped from the cab of the truck. Wearing a Nike sweatshirt, snug-fitting jeans, and steel-toed work boots, he didn't appear as out of condition as his rounded shape suggested. "Howdy, y'all. Heared 'bout yur barn-raisin' and thought ya might could use some help."

"Ain't raisin' a barn," disagreed one of

the boys. "We's raisin' us a church."

"Even better," exclaimed the man. "M'daddy were a preacher and I always been partial to churches. Now, you boys doin' the raisin' ya 'selves or be there grownups around?"

"We're up here," yelled Angela.

The man followed the sound to the top of the hill. "Now why'd ya want ta go'n build a church all the way up there?"

Angela laughed and started down the hill toward the man.

"You jist stay where ya are, young lady," he shouted. "I bin climbin' in'n'outta these hollers all m'life. One more ain't gonna kill me."

Young lady? Had he just called her *Young lady?*

By the time the man reached the top of the hill, Steve and Gilberto were standing next to Angela waiting to meet the man who drove the noisy truck.

Steve extended his hand. "I'm Steve Miller, the pastor of this church."

The man wiped his hands on his jeans and reciprocated. "Glad ta meetcha, preacher. I be Otis Langtree. Own Langtree Lumber in town. Brought m'biggest boom truck, but I'm not sure I'll be able to get 'er up the hill."

Steve looked down at the truck. "Nice rig. What's under the hood?"

"A Cummins NTC350 diesel." Otis seemed surprised to be asked the question. "Ya' familiar with it?"

"Yup," replied Steve. "I was a truck mechanic before I became a preacher."

"Well, I'll be . . . a truck mechanic turned preacher. Guess God works in mysterious ways, don't He?"

"Yes, He does." Steve scratched his head and grinned. "You know, it's been a pretty long time since I drove anything that big, but if you don't mind, I'd like to try to get it up the hill for you."

"Have at 'er, Preacher. Here's the keys." Otis tossed the keys to Steve and watched as he descended the hill.

Steve climbed into the truck, started the engine, and effortlessly and noiselessly drove away.

"Hey," shouted Otis, "where's he goin' wid m'truck?"

"I don't know." Angela craned her neck to see where Steve might have headed but both he and the truck were already out of sight.

A few minutes later, one of the workers yelled that he heard the sound of a truck coming up the opposite side of the hill.

"Do you think it is Steve?" asked Gilberto.

"I hope so," replied Angela. "Otherwise we're going to have to buy this man a new truck."

The yellow truck and trailer chugged up the hill and came to rest alongside the church.

"Now, how'd you get up here?" howled Otis.

"The back way," chuckled Steve. "That's how we got all this other stuff up here." He waved his hands indicating the stacks of lumber, shingles and windows. Handing the keys back to Otis, he added, "She's a little sloppy in second. You might want to get'er looked at."

"I'll do just that," replied Otis with conviction.

After accepting a bottle of water from one of the gofers, Otis gave Steve a quick lesson in operating the boom. "First thing you want to do is make sure your load is balanced. If it ain't, you could tip the whole kit and caboodle over and go rolling back down that hill you brought 'er up. Oh yeah, and always wear a hardhat."

Steve quickly donned a hat and listened attentively to Otis. Within an hour, he was running circles around the ridge, picking up stacks of lumber and moving them from one place to another. When it came time to raise the first wall into place, he turned the rig and hardhat over to Otis. "You go first. I wouldn't want to wreck everyone's hard work."

Without setting foot on the truck step, Otis hoisted himself into the cab, crunched the gearshift into low and rolled toward J.B. and his sons who were hammering the last studs into the framed wall. Maneuvering the vehicle into place, he moved the outriggers to stabilize the truck, lowered the boom and grabbed the wall with a hook. As the wall was lifted from the church floor, J.B. and the boys heeded Otis' warning, and holding on to the long ropes tied to each end of the wall frame, stood clear just in case a sudden gust of wind caused the wall to sway. Which, of course, didn't happen. Otis slowly raised the wall, wiggled it to the edge of the flooring, and held it steady while J.B. and his oldest son secured it in place. The entire procedure was repeated with the remaining walls and by noon the church was ready for a roof.

Forewarned that Angela had planned a sumptuous barbecue, everyone kept working. Doors and windows were fitted into rough openings, roof trusses attached to the framed walls, and plywood sheathing nailed to the trusses. Except for roofing felt, shingles and paint, the church was finished.

Angela stood back and admired the building. It was larger than the original church, but that was good because the congregation was growing rapidly. There were more windows, but that was also good because it meant there would be more sunlight. And, since there were only two steps up to the front door, it would be easier for the older parishioners to get in and out. All in all, the new church was going to be wonderful. But, looking closer, she noticed something was missing.

Calling Steve over, she whispered in his ear. "What about a bell tower?"

Steve smiled reassuringly. "Don't worry, Angela, we'll have one."

The twinkle in Steve's eyes gave Angela the impression he was holding something back. But, even though she wanted to find out what it was, she had a horde of hungry people clamoring for food.

"We want food," bellowed two young boys. "We want food."

Angela shooed the boys away and hurried toward Pam's truck where she and Gelah were unloading boxes and covered dishes from the truck bed.

When Gelah had first heard Angela was planning a barbecue, she'd insisted on being in charge. "I might not be able to swing a hammer, but I've been cooking for crowds pretty much my whole life. How does fried chicken, baked beans, cornbread, collard greens, and strawberry-rhubarb cobbler sound?"

"Like a lot of work," Angela had responded. "But if you're up to it, it would sure make my life a lot easier." Now she was glad she'd agreed, because looking at the amount of food coming off the back of Pam's truck, she knew there was no way she would have been able to cook that much . . . even with Gilberto's help.

Instead of setting up tables inside the church, J.B. insisted they be kept outside. "Wouldn't wanna drop anythin' on that new floor 'fore the preacher blesses it." His sons arranged the tables perpendicular to the front of the church so that everyone would have an unobstructed view of their marvelous achievement.

When all the food was laid out, Steve climbed the two steps to the front door, faced his congregation, and raised his hands. A few moans and mutters were stifled as hungry workers grudgingly lowered partially eaten chicken legs to the paper plates in front of them.

"I know you think I'm going to say grace

before we eat," announced Steve, "but I'm going to let someone else do it today. Florence . . . would you mind leading us in prayer?"

Little Florence reached out and grabbed the hands of the people on either side of her, who in turn joined hands with the people sitting next to them. Lowering her head, she took a deep breath and shouted, "Look out lips, look out gums, look out stomach, here it comes."

Everyone responded with a resounding "Amen" and quickly got down to the serious business of eating. Twenty minutes later, all that was left of twenty fried chickens, five gallons of baked beans, ten trays of corn bread, and a whole mess of collard greens were bones, crumbs, and messy bean pots. Pam and Monica placed cobblers and a giant tub of Cool Whip on each table. Within moments that, too, was devoured.

Steve rose from his seat at the table closest to the church doors and raised his hands again. "Today has been a wonderful day," he said. "God blessed us with beautiful weather and provided us with a bountiful feast. We all worked hard and have rebuilt His church. Let us give thanks for all He has given us and for all the unknown blessings still to come." He started to sit down but abruptly rose again. "Oh yeah . . . I almost forgot. We'll continue to hold Sunday services at J.B. Walton's barn until we get the new roof up and bring the pews back here, but the more hands we have, the quicker the work will go. So . . . how about we all meet back here next Saturday?"

Some people nodded in agreement, others shook their heads and grumbled as they got up from the tables and walked toward their trucks. Looking at their faces, Angela knew most of them would be back. These were hard-working, dependable people who always finished whatever they started. She was proud to be part of their community and wanted to thank each and every one of them for everything they'd done. Noticing Gelah cleaning off one of the tables, she rushed to her friend and wrapped her arms around her. "I love you," she cried out.

Looking somewhat surprised, Gelah steadied herself and looked directly into Angela's tear-filled eyes. "Well, my goodness. What brought that on?"

"Nothing," said Angela breathlessly. "Everything. You are a wonderful person, and I just wanted to tell you how happy I am that we're friends."

"Well, I'm happy, too, Angela. Now can you please help me load these things into

Pam's truck? I need to get home before dark."

Angela knew Gelah wasn't one to express her feelings openly. Granted, they'd hugged a time or two when the occasion called for it, but evidently a church raising didn't justify a public display of affection. Maybe it had something to do with raising so many foster children. It must have been hard to bring children into her home, love them and then let them go. She had let Rebecca go before she ever got to know her. How would she feel if she had to let her, or Dominick, go now?

After helping Gelah clear the rest of the tables and pack everything into Pam's truck bed, Angela kissed her friend on the cheek and said good-bye. Then, since Gilberto had left earlier to drive little Florence and her family home, she decided to walk home.

Even though daylight-saving time meant an extra hour before the sun set, the shadows along the road were already deepening as Angela headed toward home. From what she could still see, wildflowers were popping up all over the moss-covered ground beneath the trees. Their fragrance filled the air with an indescribable delight. Overhead, several birds twittered as they searched the trees for comfortable night roosts. Until a couple of years ago, walking alone down a lonely country road would have frightened her. She would have jumped at every little noise. She would have peered around trees and rocks to make sure a boogeyman wasn't waiting to jump out at her. Or she might even have run. As if that would have done any good. But that was a couple of years ago when her life was still in turmoil. In those days, she was even afraid of her own shadow. Now, except for the occasional copperhead, she knew there was nothing along this road to fear.

Stopping at the mailbox, she picked up the mail. There was a bill from the telephone company, a flyer from the co-op, and a letter with a strange-looking stamp and postmark. The letter was from her redheaded friend, Katherine — all the way from Cuba. Now, if that wasn't reason enough to run, what was?

Gizmo, probably wishing he could open it, was peacefully asleep in front of the refrigerator when Angela rushed into the house. She had filled his bowl with dry food before she left, but as usual, he seemed to be holding out for something better. *How did he always know,* she wondered. She placed the mail on the kitchen table, opened the refrigerator, removed two hot dogs from their wrapper, cut them into small pieces, and added them to the dog's bowl. Just like the workers at the church, the dog gulped down his food, licked the sides and bottom of the bowl, and looked to Angela for more.

"That's all for now, buddy. If you want to keep up with Dominick and Boomer when we go down to see them, you're gonna have to lose some weight."

As if understanding every word his mistress had spoken, Gizmo lay back in front of the refrigerator, placed his head between his paws and sighed mournfully.

Sitting down at the kitchen table, Angela pushed the co-op flyer and telephone bill aside then ripped open Katherine's letter and began reading:

Hey, Goat Lady,

How are things going? You tired of country living yet? Knowing you, probably not. You always were something of a hayseed, but I love you anyway.

Living in Cuba has been, how should I put this? Different? Everyone drives old American cars, the men spend countless hours playing dominoes in the plaza, hardly anyone speaks English, and those who do have such heavy accents I can't understand a word they're saying. As an

American, I am treated like royalty, while Mongo is treated like a poor relative. Which, truth be known, he is. His family is nice, but they live in very old houses that they can't afford to repair. If I go shopping for something, I pay one price. If Mongo or someone in his family shops for the same item, they have to pay a higher price. Everything he does is regulated by the government, but he never complains because he is afraid he might get thrown into prison. The scenery here is beautiful and the weather isn't much different from Florida's. Sometimes I feel like I'm back at Egret Cove — other times I know I'm not.

But, enough about my life. I know you're working on restoring Steve's old church and remember you said everything, including the bell tower, was destroyed. What a shame considering how hard the children worked to buy the bell. Anyway, I wanted to do something to help, so I went on the Internet (had to go to one of the hotels to get access) and found a little something you might be able to use. It's not much, but I think you'll like it. I had to jump through hoops to get this thing ordered and shipped (it's coming from Pennsylvania), but you and Steve are worth the effort. By the way . . . is he still so gorgeous?

I hope you are doing well. Please write when you can, kiss Gil for me, and yeah, give that mangy dog of yours a big smooch, too — YUK.

I love you and miss you. Your BFF,
                                                    Katherine

Angela read the letter again . . . and again . . . and again.

CHAPTER 15
ON THE ROAD . . . AGAIN

Getting the baby goats to Alabama turned out to be more difficult than first imagined. For starters, it was raining when Angela and Gilberto loaded them into the truck at four a.m. and the animals' wet bodies gave off a stench strangely reminiscent of decaying fish and day-old beer. Bored after spending five minutes away from their playmates, the juveniles quickly devised a game that could only be called *Tailgate Tag.* Taking turns, they reared up on their hind legs, lowered their heads and rammed into the truck's tailgate, sending shock waves up to the passengers in the cab.

Before exiting the hollow, Gilberto stopped the truck, walked around to the rear, and checked the tailgate to make sure it was securely locked. "We would not want them to fall out on the highway," he stated, "would we?"

Angela peered through the window separating the truck cab from the bed. "Do you think it would help if we put Gizmo in with them?"

Gilberto shook his head in disbelief. "I thought you loved that dog."

"I do," replied Angela, "but maybe his presence would calm them down. You know how good he is with Bucky."

"Sì, sì, but Bucky is a friend. These goats are . . . how do you say? . . . little monsters."

Realizing her husband was probably right, Angela tried to ignore the gyrations taking place in the back of the truck. Nevertheless, as they approached the first rest stop on the Interstate, she begged Gilberto to stop. Grabbing the two leashes and leather collars she'd brought along, she got out and walked around to the rear of the truck.

Gilberto followed. "What are you going to do?" he asked.

"Take the kids for a walk," she said. "Maybe a little fresh air and exercise will wear them out." When she reached the tailgate, she raised the window portion, reached in, and monitoring their every movement, fastened a collar around each goat's neck. Next, she clipped a leash to each collar and began to lower the bottom of the tailgate. Watching from the cab,

Gizmo whined, as if asking, "What about me?"

Distracted by a large semitrailer rolling through the parking area, Angela took her eyes off the goats for a split second. That was all they needed.

Launching from the rear of the pickup, they flew past Angela, tore loose from her hold, raced across the tarmac, and headed straight toward the pet exercise area. A startled driver slammed on his brakes as the goats passed in front of his vehicle. An elderly woman in the pet area clutched a nervous Chihuahua to her chest and made a mad dash for her car. Two teenage boys sitting at one of the picnic tables saw what was happening, jumped up, and took off after the runaway goats.

Looking like a kid on a Slip'n Slide, one of the boys slid across the grassy surface of the pet area, grabbed the rear legs of one of the kids, and held on for dear life as the goat struggled to break free. The other boy ripped off his windbreaker, threw it over the second kid's head, and brought the animal to an abrupt standstill.

When Angela reached the boys, the first thing she asked was, "Are you all right?"

"Them your goats?" asked the larger boy. His hair was carrot red, even redder than

Katherine's, and his face was peppered with large orange freckles. If he'd been wearing a straw hat and rolled-up jeans, he could have been mistaken for Tom Sawyer.

"Yes," she replied breathlessly. "Thanks for catching them. Are you boys okay?"

"We're fi-fi-fi-fine," stuttered the second boy.

"They took off so fast I couldn't catch up with them," said Angela. Getting down on her knees, she checked each animal to make sure it hadn't suffered any injury. While she was doing that, Gilberto appeared with Gizmo in tow.

"Have they been hurt?" he asked.

"No," she sighed, "but if these boys hadn't stopped them, they might have been. What if they'd run out on the Interstate?"

"And who are these fine young men?" asked Gilberto.

The Tom Sawyer look-alike extended his hand to Gilberto. "I'm John, and this here's m'brother Bob."

Except for fewer freckles, the younger boy was the mirror image of his brother. In fact, he could have passed for Huck Finn. Angela wondered what the boys were doing at the rest area. "Where are your parents?" she asked. Surely, they weren't here alone.

"Dad's in the john," replied the boy

named Bob. "We ate dinner at a tr-u-u-uck stop last night, and he-ee-ee's not feeling too good."

"We've got some ginger ale in our truck," offered Angela. "Do you think he'd like one?"

"Nah," replied John. "He'll be all right." Looking down at the baby goats, he asked, "What're their names?"

"Adam and Eve," she replied. "We're taking them down to my daughter in Alabama so she can start a herd."

"Neat," shouted Bob. "I got ra-a-a-abits back home."

"And where is that?" asked Gilberto.

"Ohio," replied John proudly. "We're goin' downta North Carolina ta visit our gran'parents." Looking toward the main building, the boy noticed his father standing next to their truck. "Com'on, Bobby, Dad's ready ta go."

"How can we ever thank you?" asked Angela.

"Aah, t'weren't nuttin," mumbled John.

Not knowing what else to do, Angela hugged Bob while Gilberto shook hands with John. Staring at the twenty-dollar bill Gilberto had slipped him, the older boy quickly objected. "I kain't take this."

"Yes you can," insisted Gilberto. "Stop at

the next town and buy your father some cottage cheese and bananas. It will help him feel better."

"Okay," muttered John as he tugged at his brother's arm.

"Thanks again," shouted Angela as the boys walked away.

John waved but didn't look back. When he reached his father's truck, he and Bob climbed in, the father backed out of the parking area, and they disappeared down the road.

"I'm so glad they were here," sighed Angela as she brushed some silvery strands of hair from her eyes.

"As am I," agreed Gilberto. "But now we must leave, amore. We have a long day ahead."

Angela loaded the goats back into the truck, gave them fresh water, and patted their heads before closing the tailgate and climbing in next to Gilberto. "Well, I guess we're ready," she said. "Alabama . . . here we come."

After their ill-gotten freedom, the goats seemed to settle down. Either that or the monotonous drone of tires on pavement made them sleepy. Regardless of the reason, shortly after leaving the rest area, they curled up in the hay and went to sleep. At one point Angela even thought she heard one of them snoring. But she could have been mistaken. Maybe it had just been Gizmo who was stretched out across the rear seat.

Fourteen long hours after leaving West Virginia, Gilberto parked his truck alongside the newly erected goat shed that was now part of Mariposa Landing. As Angela prepared to unload the goats, her daughter ran up to greet her.

"How was the trip, Mom?" asked Rebecca.

"Interesting," laughed Angela as she and Rebecca hugged. "Very, very interesting."

"Really? Well, let's get these animals unloaded, then you can tell me all about it. Are you hungry?"

"Famished," replied Angela. "We had sandwiches and fruit, but something about road trips always makes me hungry."

"I wasn't sure what time you'd get in, so I put a jug of sun tea and a big bowl of pasta salad in your refrigerator. I even baked a batch of snicker doodles this morning."

Mother and daughter settled the animals into their new home and then headed for the little house Dominick referred to as the *Little House on the Bayou.* It had only two rooms — a kitchen, living, and dining room in one area, and a bedroom and bath in the other — but it was more beautifully decorated than any hotel room Angela had ever seen, including the one she and Gilberto stayed in at the Bayview Manor.

A watercolor likeness of the bay hung above a sea foam green pillow-back sofa that looked out a picture window at the real thing. Below the window, a coffee table draped in a lace table runner was almost totally covered by the heart-shaped leaves of a healthy philodendron.

On the same wall as the first picture window, a second window also looked out upon the bay, but instead of a coffee table, it was accented with an oak drop leaf table and two matching chairs. In the middle of the table, a small decoupaged plaque etched with the words *The Love Between a Mother and Daughter Grows Forever,* rested on a silver easel placed atop the Circle of Life doily Gelah had crocheted for Rebecca.

Directly across from the second window, a stove, refrigerator, sink, and cabinets occupied a small alcove. An old-fashioned glass percolator sat on the stove with a basket of gourmet coffees, teas, and the cookies Rebecca baked on the adjoining countertop. A green and gold braid rug covered the highly polished pine flooring.

Angela wondered if the rug had been hand-made.

The room behind the sofa contained a comfortable-looking bed covered in a soft green comforter, two night tables and lamps, a dresser, and an oak rocker with a crocheted afghan draped over the back rungs. On the wall backing the kitchen, the bathroom was outfitted with a commode, a clawfoot tub, a pedestal bowl sink with bronze faucets and a small walk-in closet.

All in all, the little cottage was cozy, comfortable, and much more than Angela had ever expected. "Who did all of this?" she asked.

Rebecca beamed. If she'd been wearing suspenders she probably would have hooked her thumbs behind them. "Your grandson. He did all the shopping and color-coordinated everything himself. He even got down on his hands and knees and waxed the floor. Said everything had to be perfect so his Grams would keep coming back."

"That's sweet. Where is he, anyway?" From the bedroom window, Angela could see the parking area where Dominick kept his truck. The truck was there but the boy was nowhere in sight.

"He's out training with Jack. Even though it's only a 10K, he wants to be in good shape for his first race."

Angela sat on the edge of the bed and bounced. The mattress was firm but cushy — just the way she and Gilberto liked it. "How many miles is a 10K?"

"A little over six," replied Rebecca.

"And a marathon is what . . . 25 miles?"

"26 point 2 to be exact. Dominick wants to do the *Life Without Limits* half marathon up in Florence in October, then the Pensacola full marathon in November."

"Do you think he'll be ready?"

"He is now," chuckled Rebecca. "Jack paces him with a 10 speed bicycle and says he has trouble keeping up."

"Out of curiosity . . . what does Jack wear when he and Dominick go out?"

"He wears black racing shorts and a red jersey with the number forty-two on the front. He says it makes him look and feel like Dario Franchitti."

"The Indy-500 winner?"

"That's the one. Do you follow NASCAR?"

"Just the Indy," replied Angela. "I began listening to it when I started going camping after my divorce, and I've been hooked ever since. Memorial Day just wouldn't be the same without it."

"Without what?" asked Gilberto as he carried two suitcases into the room.

"The Indianapolis 500," said Rebecca, grabbing one of the suitcases and setting it inside the closet.

Following his daughter-in-law's lead, Gilberto placed the second suitcase next to the first. "Ah, sì. Angela and I listened to it last year."

A wistful smile softened Angela's face. Last Memorial Day she and the children from Camp Gizmo had been hard at work on their garden. She remembered how carefully the children had planted the seeds, watched them sprout, and kept the tender young plants watered and weeded throughout the summer. She remembered their faces as they'd taken their crops to the farmers' market and their pride at being able to put money aside for a new church bell. She even remembered the day the bell had been delivered. Those had been such wonderful days. By the grace of God, there would be more like them in her future.

A loud tap on the window dissolved Angela's daydream. Rising from the bed, she went to the window and looked out. A sweaty Dominick smiled up at her.

Opening the window, Angela leaned out and tousled her grandson's damp hair. "How ya doing big guy?"

"Pretty good," bragged Dominick. "Jack gave up on me about an hour ago, but I kept going. Even so, I probably did thirty miles today."

"Wow, that's great," exclaimed Angela. "Why don't you go around to the front and come inside? Your mom says there's cold tea in the refrigerator."

Dominick pointed down at his racing chair. "Can't. This thing won't fit through the door." The racing chair was maraschino-cherry-red with two large disc-like wheels angled in toward the passenger cage, and a smaller, spoked wheel an arm's length down the elongated tubular fork. Leaning forward from a kneeling position, Dominick rested his hands on what appeared to be the controls. He wore a white baseball cap turned backwards and a red vest, but no shirt. Sweat poured down his face, and when he removed the cap to wipe his forehead, his hair popped skyward in small, tight curls.

"Okay, then. Meet us out front and we'll bring the tea to you."

Before Angela could close the window, Dominick disappeared around the corner of the house. Within seconds, the terrifying sounds of a dogfight filled the small house.

Gilberto was first out of the door, Rebecca

followed him, and Angela brought up the rear. Standing on the porch, they all broke into laughter as they watched Gizmo and Boomer cavort around Dominick and his racing chair. First, the dogs went in one direction. Then, rapidly shifting gears, they turned around and went the opposite way. The whole time, they barked and snapped at each other, but never attempted to make contact.

"Well," laughed Rebecca, "I see our dogs have met."

Angela grinned and nodded her head. "Yup. Kinda looks that way."

Dominick calmed down the dogs and turned to Angela. "I'll take that tea now," he said.

Angela and Rebecca went back into the house, filled four glasses with ice and tea, then carried them outside to Dominick and Gilberto. Dominick was petting Gizmo when Angela handed him his tea. " 'At's a nice dog," he said. "What kind is it?"

"Part Australian sheepdog, part Licksit hound," replied Angela.

Dominick furrowed his brow. "What'sa Licksit hound?"

"You know . . . anything he sees . . . he licks it."

Dominick rolled his eyes and groaned.

"Are you ready for your big race on Sunday?" asked Angela.

"Yeah, but this one is no big deal . . . it's only a 10K," replied Dominick. "This time of year there aren't many races because of the heat. But there are a couple of full marathons next fall that I've already signed up for."

Rebecca's jaw dropped. "You have? When?"

"Last week," admitted Dominick. "Jack helped me with the paperwork."

"Well, I wish you would have told me."

"What's the big deal, Mom? You knew I was gonna."

Hoping to avoid the inevitable, Angela quickly changed the subject. "So . . . are you gonna carb up tomorrow night?"

Dominick's eyes gleamed with surprise. "How'd you know about that?"

"I've been surfing the Internet at the library."

"Yeah, well you haven't surfed enough. Used to be that guys ate big pasta dinners the night before a race, but they've discovered that just loads you down. If you're gonna carb up, you gotta start a couple days ahead, then taper down before the race."

"Is that right?" Angela smiled. In a very short time, Dominick had found a new interest, pursued it, and obviously learned everything there was to know about it. Her choice of books hadn't been that far off base after all.

"Wanna help me train tomorrow?"

Without hesitating, Angela jumped at the chance. "Of course. What do I have to do?"

After explaining the duties of a trainer, Dominick narrowed his eyes and asked his grandmother the crucial question. "You can ride a bike . . . can't you?"

Angela smirked and nodded her head. "There are some things you never forget no matter how old you get."

The following morning, Angela slipped into a pair of Bermuda shorts and a tee shirt and walked the short distance across the road to her daughter's house. Dominick was in his front yard polishing his chair. He pointed toward a large tree, which judging by the shape of its leaves, appeared to be a southern magnolia. Leaning against the tree's scaly trunk was a fat-tired, fuchsia and white bicycle with a pink wicker basket hanging from the upright handlebars. "That's my mom's old bike," he said. "She used to use it to go to the library, but hasn't touched it in the last year or two. I oiled the chain and put air in the tires so you should be good to go."

Angela inspected the bicycle. Looking straight out of the 1960s, it had a 3-speed shifter on the right half of the handlebar and hand brakes at both ends. An extra large chain guard enclosed the non-sprocketed chain, and an exceptionally narrow saddle perched high on the seat post.

Tossing a bottle of water into Angela's pink basket, Dominick informed her they would start out slowly.

Well, that's a good thing, she thought.

The first hour went well. She shifted through the gears effortlessly, applied the handbrakes expertly, and maneuvered the curves as if she'd been doing it all of her life. Which, of course, she had. Dominick had led her off the farm, down a steep hill and along the shore. At one point it seemed as if she were flying. After pulling into a quiet bayside park to take what she considered a well-deserved break, she sipped water and looked around.

Gentle waves splashed over fist-sized rocks lining the shore. Three white seagulls argued over the remains of a fish. A long-legged blue heron waited patiently in the shallows. The deep turquoise of the sky above and the scent of what . . . crape myrtle? . . . made her want to take her shoes off and go wading in the water.

Fifteen minutes later, Dominick asked if she was ready to head back. Even though she wished they could stay longer, she recapped her water bottle, placed it back in the wicker basket and nodded. "Sure, let's do it."

The minute they exited the park, Angela made a disheartening revelation — the trip home was going to be . . . *up hill.*

CHAPTER 16
A DAY TO REMEMBER

The only thing Angela wanted to do Sunday morning was stay in bed. During the night she'd experienced no less than four charley horses — one in each calf, one in her right thigh, and one in her left foot. There might have been more, but Gilberto had massaged her legs, and instead of continued pain, all she experienced were tender dreams about running through the corn with her handsome husband. Even so, when she finally awoke, her legs felt like iron barbells. Luckily she and Gilberto had gone to church the night before, otherwise she would never have been able to genuflect in front of the altar.

Pulling herself into an upright position and shoving a pillow between her back and the headboard, she sighed as Gilberto offered her a steaming mug of coffee. "Isn't caffeine one of the things that *cause* charley horses?"

"Sì," he replied. "But this is decaffeinated coffee. I added hot, not steamed, milk. Taste it to see if you like it."

Angela took a cautious sip. "Ummm. It has an almost chocolaty flavor."

"Oui, oui, mademoiselle. Zat is de chi-cor-EE."

Gulping to keep from spitting coffee all over Dominick's beautiful new comforter, Angela roared with laughter. "French? When did you start speaking French?"

Gilberto scowled. "No, no, mademoiselle. Zat is not French, zat is *Cajun.* Jist like da coff-EE."

Angela snickered and took another sip of the coffee. "This wouldn't be from Café du Monde, would it?"

"But of course."

"Does that mean you also made beignets?"

"All I have to do is heat the oil. I was waiting until you arose."

Angela laboriously swung her legs over the side of the bed. Every muscle in her body, not just those in her legs, ached. What had made her think she could keep up with her grandson? Pride? Vanity? Stupidity? Whatever it was, she vowed never to let anything like that foolhardy bike ride happen again. Unless, of course, Dominick needed someone to ride along with him.

By the time she finished her shower and slipped into a loose-fitting sundress and sandals, Angela felt completely revived. Bouncing into the kitchen, she wrapped her arms around Gilberto who was dousing a batch of deep-fried beignets with copious amounts of powdered sugar.

"What is the hug for?" asked Gilberto.

"For being such a wonderful husband," she replied kissing his cheek.

Tapping his right shoulder, the one farthest from her, Angela snatched a beignet from beneath Gilberto's left hand and popped it into her mouth. When he turned to look at her she tried to conceal the powdery treat filling out her cheeks.

"What have you done?" he asked pretending to be angry.

"Nuffin' . . ." she muttered. Small puffs of powdered sugar escaped with each syllable.

A gentle knock at the screen door caught them both laughing hysterically. Desperately trying to wipe away any telltale sugar from her lips, Angela walked the few steps to the door and found Dominick staring up at her. "I'm heading out for the race . . . you gonna be there?"

"Of course," she replied. "When does it start?"

"At nine. Jack is taking me down now, and

Mom will follow in a little while." Dominick stretched to look around Angela into the kitchen. "Is that beignets I smell?"

"Yes, it is," replied Gilberto. "Would you like to come in and have some?"

"Better not, they might slow me down."

"So where do we go?" asked Angela.

"The race starts at the park we were at yesterday and then follows the bay up to the municipal pier in town. You could watch from any place along the way, but it would probably be more fun to be at the finish line. That's where Mom will be waiting. Maybe you could pack up a couple of those beignets so I could eat them after the race."

"That is a marvelous idea," said Gilberto. "But I will not put the sugar on them until you cross the line. That way, they will not become too gummy."

"Thanks, Gil. Oh, and by the way, Grams . . . you might want to check a mirror before you leave. It looks like you have a white moustache."

Angela shot a hand to her upper lip. When she pulled it away, it was covered with powdered sugar. "Good grief, Gil, why didn't you tell me?"

"Because I planned to kiss it off, amore."

"Mush," exclaimed Dominick as he backed away from the door. "I'm not sticking around for any of that." Shaking his head, he rolled away from the little house and toward Jack's waiting truck. In the back of the truck, the cherry-red racing chair was held in place by several bungee cords. In the front seat, an eager Boomer awaited his master.

Placing her hands on her hips, Angela turned to Gilberto. "I should be mad at you," she huffed.

"But you are not . . . are you?"

The smirk on Gilberto's face was too hard to resist. Raising her hands from her hips, Angela grabbed a freshly powdered beignet and rubbed it all over his mouth, his cheeks, and even his hair. While trying to escape his wife's relentless onslaught, Gilberto picked up one of the pastries and followed suit. Within seconds, they were chasing each other around the little house like children in a playground. Another knock at the door quickly brought them back to their senses.

"Can I play too?" A grinning Rebecca stood at the front door.

Angela froze in her tracks and attempted to hide the remains of her assault weapon behind her back. "Rebecca . . . please . . . come in. We were just . . ."

"No need to explain, Mom," said Rebecca. "David and I once had a tomato war."

"Tomatoes?" giggled Angela. "What made you choose tomatoes?"

"It's a long story," replied Rebecca. "I'll tell you all about it some time. But for now, how about you two go get cleaned up, and I'll drive you down to the pier?"

Angela examined her hands and Gilberto's face. "This may take a while. Maybe we should just meet you down there."

"Okay," agreed Rebecca. "But don't take too long. I think there are going to be a lot of people, and I want to make sure we get a good spot."

Thirty minutes later, the freshly-scrubbed Angela and Gilberto pulled into the parking area adjoining the pier. The first time they saw the pier had been last winter when they came to meet Rebecca. Had that only been five months ago? So much had happened since then. They'd met and grown to love Angela's daughter and grandson, helped bring a new generation of goats into the world, two of which they transported all the way from West Virginia to Alabama, and were now getting ready to watch a young man, who'd never walked, run his first race. Angela wondered what other miracles God was hiding up His sleeve.

Rebecca waved from the far side of the parking lot where a yellow *Finish Line* banner had been stretched across the narrow passage leading to the long wooden pier. Off to one side, a larger-than-life digital clock was ticking off the minutes and seconds since the race began.

About fifty people had gathered to watch the runners come in. According to Dominick, the wheelchair racers, of which there were four, would be the first wave to leave the starting point and arrive at the finishing point. The foot racers would follow. Although some experienced racers were expected to finish in as little as thirty or forty minutes, Dominick said he'd be happy if he did it in anything under an hour.

Raising a disposable camera, Rebecca shot Angela and Gilberto's picture as they approached her vantage point about two feet from the finish line clock. "You two clean up well," she tittered.

Angela crossed her eyes and puffed out her cheeks. "You really think so?"

"Absolutely," replied Rebecca as she took another snapshot. "That's why I took your picture. I want everyone to see just how beautiful my mother and her husband are when they not covered in powdered sugar."

"Why, thank you, ma'am," drawled Gilberto.

Peering over the top of her amber-tinted sunglasses, Rebecca turned toward Gilberto. "Where did you find this guy?"

"In a trailer park in south Florida," replied Angela smugly.

"Well, take me there, please. I want one just like him."

A sudden roar brought an end to the mother-daughter banter as one, two, three wheelchairs swung around a flowering rose garden and sped toward the finish line. The first chair was yellow, the second blue, and the third silver. Where was Dominick?

As if on cue, the red chair came into view. With his head bent low and his arms almost a blur, Dominick overtook the silver chair and crossed the line at exactly 30 minutes, 15 seconds. The first place winner had finished in 29 minutes, 52 seconds — second place had come in at 30 minutes, 10 seconds.

Before Angela or Rebecca could reach him, a cute teenage girl, dressed in Daisy Dukes and a pink crop top, rushed up, threw her arms around Dominick's bulging shoulders and planted a big kiss on his sweaty face.

"Who's that?" questioned Angela.

"Marisol," replied Rebecca. "The new girlfriend."

"What happened to Esperanza?"

"Thrown out like last week's newspaper."

The tone in Rebecca's voice suggested disapproval, but Angela thought better than to ask any more questions. Grabbing Rebecca and Gilberto's arms and pulling them along behind, she pushed through the crowd and headed for Dominick. By the time they reached him, Marisol had removed his baseball cap and was tying a black paisley bandana around his head.

"Hey," he shouted, "did you see how I pulled ahead of that guy in the silver chair?" He was out of breath and overheated but filled with the exhilaration of accomplishing more than anyone, including himself, had expected.

"Yes, we did," replied Rebecca as she patted her grandson on the back. "We're so proud of you."

Stepping back from Dominick's racing chair, Marisol hung her head and studied her pink flowered flip-flops. "Buenos Días, Mrs. Taylor," she muttered.

"And to you, Marisol." Angela's icy manner showed no sign of thawing. "Did your brother come today?"

"No, Mrs. Taylor, Raúl did not come

today." The girl never raised her eyes.

Putting two and two together, Angela deduced that Marisol's brother was probably the same young man who'd offered her and Dominick that offensive pulque the day they drove down to the bay. That could mean only one thing — Raúl was trouble. Hoping to dodge a brewing storm, she bent down and kissed Dominick's cheek. "Congratulations, big guy. How about we all head over to the White Seagull and celebrate with some pecan pancakes?"

"Gil said he was going to bring me some beignets," objected Dominick.

"I am so sorry," apologized Gilberto. "We left the house in such a hurry that I forgot to bring them."

"Besides," said Rebecca. "We have reservations for an early supper at Bellingrath Gardens."

"What is Bellingrath Gardens?" asked Gilberto.

"It's a sixty-five acre estate on the other side of the bay. The gardens are said to be the most beautiful in Alabama, if not the entire United States. There are magnificent rose gardens, butterfly gardens, formal Japanese gardens, a boardwalk into the bayou, and a beautiful lake surrounded by all sorts of flowering trees and shrubs. Every year the Mobile Symphony Youth Orchestra puts on a concert and picnic supper for Mother's Day. I invited Jack and Vesta to come along. Jack has a big van and offered to drive. We're supposed to be at his place by eleven."

"Can I run home and shower first?" asked Dominick.

"Well, I should hope so," replied Rebecca adamantly. Turning to Marisol she added, "I made the reservation for six people, but if you would like to join us, I could probably change it to seven."

Still not raising her head, Marisol courteously declined. "My family has made other plans."

Jack's nine-passenger van was equipped with a 26-inch flat screen television, surround sound, twin sunroofs, reclining seats, a GPS tracker, and a compact refrigerator filled with ice water, Mountain Dew, and raspberry tea. In anticipation of the 30-mile road trip, Vesta had prepared watercress sandwiches, deviled eggs, and ham-and-cheese rollups, all of which were packed away in the red and white Thermos cooler wedged between her feet.

Rather than taking the quickest route, Jack drove the van up along the Eastern Shore, followed the Causeway across the bay, and detoured through the Mobile Historic District before heading south to the small town of Theodore. When he pulled into the Bellingrath Gardens parking lot at two o'clock, the deviled eggs, sandwiches and raspberry tea were gone, Angela and Vesta had formed an impenetrable bond, and Dominick was sound asleep.

"Do we really have to wake him?" asked Angela. "He must be tired after the race."

Rebecca laughed. "The race had nothing to do with it. Stick him in a car and he'll fall asleep within ten minutes. He's been that way since he was a baby. I guess beneath all that bravado, he's still very much a child." She gently shook Dominick's shoulder. "Come on sleepy head, rise and shine."

Dominick yawned, stretched and groggily muttered, "Are we there yet?"

"See what I mean?"

Bellingrath Gardens surpassed Angela's expectations by a long shot. The gardens weren't just gardens, they were tapestries woven of pink, yellow, white, and purple gifts from Heaven. The boardwalk crossing into the bayou wasn't a mere walkway, it was a transport into another dimension. Instead of just being surrounded by flowering trees and shrubs, the lake provided a welcome respite from the outside world. An exotic blend of fragrances drifted on the gentle breeze that cooled the otherwise still air. A chorus of unidentified birds kept time with the classical music being piped through inconspicuous speakers. Small children held their parents' hands and admired the bees and butterflies drifting from blossom to blossom, while two ruby-throated hummingbirds hovered over a trumpet vine. Everywhere she turned, Angela found something new and astonishing to delight her senses.

After touring the fifteen-room house built by the estate's original owners, the group headed over to the Live Oak Plaza where linen-covered tables had been set up under the trees. Getting in line behind a handful of people, they picked up their boxed suppers, purchased three bottles of Pinot Grigio and sought out a table. Although Dominick seemed anxious to tear open his box, Rebecca slowed him down by informing him, "Slow down, Dominick, this isn't a race."

Dominick immediately pushed his dinner box away, grabbed a plastic wineglass and held it out to be filled. Jack poured wine into all the glasses except Dominick's, then stood up and raised his in a toast.

"Today is a special day, not just because our friend, son, and grandson has run his first race, coming in at third place I may add, but also because it is Mother's Day, and we have three of God's greatest creations among us."

Vesta smiled, Rebecca sighed, and Angela fought back tears.

"Our mothers were our first loves. They risked their lives to give us birth, they held our hands when we took our first steps, they kissed our wounds, and they mended our hearts after others broke them. Always aware of our limitations, they believed in us, they gave us hope, and they never gave up."

Gilberto hugged Angela's shoulders as tears trickled down her face.

"Please join me in telling each one of them how important they are to us, how very much we love them, and how grateful we are that God sent them to us." Jack raised his glass above his head, saluted all three mothers, and then leaned down and kissed his own.

Vesta tried to push her son away, saying he was acting like a ninny, but he laughed and kissed her again.

When congratulations had made their way around the table, Rebecca rose from her seat. "As you all know, I was raised by a loving woman who took me into her family and her heart, and it wasn't until five months ago that I met the woman who gave me life.

"That woman, of course, was Angela Fontero." She paused, inhaled deeply and placed her hand on Angela's shoulder. "For whatever reason, Angela couldn't raise me, but she followed her motherly instincts and gave me to someone who could. It was an unselfish and loving thing to do.

"That was more than forty years ago. But now she is back in my life, not simply as my biological mother, but also as my friend."

Angela rose and hugged Rebecca, Gilberto wrapped his arms around them both, Jack tried to kiss his mother again . . . unsuccessfully . . . and the orchestra played Tchaikovsky's Polonaise from Eugene Onegin as Dominick quietly mumbled, "I still want to know why she walked out."

CHAPTER 17
REBIRTH

As much as Angela enjoyed celebrating her first official Mother's Day with her daughter and grandson, she was happy to get back to West Virginia. Alabama was beautiful, but something about West Virginia grounded her. Whether it was the rolling hills, the rippling streams, the wildlife, or the people, she felt it was home — the place where her life had meaning — the place where her friends were — the place where she could relax and not feel like a tourist.

The day she and Gilberto returned to Hummingbird Ridge, Steve called. "You won't believe what Katherine sent us."

"Let me guess," she chuckled. "A subscription to Mother Earth News? A year's supply of Bag Balm? A book about building your own outhouse?"

"No . . . a bell tower. She wrote and said she was going to send one, but I thought it would just be a simple little cupola. This thing stands twenty feet tall and has a copper roof."

Steve was talking so fast and loud that Angela had to hold the telephone receiver six inches away from her ear. "That's a good thing . . . isn't it?"

"Well, yes," conceded Steve. "But it sort of overpowers our little church. Lucky it's made of vinyl, otherwise we'd have to ask Otis to bring his boom truck back out."

"When are we going to put it up?"

"That's what I wanted to talk to you about," said Steve. "Are you going to do Camp Gizmo again this year? If so, maybe getting the bell tower up could be the kids' first project. After all, they're the ones who paid for the bell."

Angela took a deep breath and exhaled it in one long sigh. "I don't know, Steve. So much has been happening lately, I haven't given it much thought." The truth was she'd thought about it — a lot — and she was worried about something going wrong. Last year's camp had been productive and good for the children, but it had ended disastrously for everyone. Repeating it might bring similar results, and now that everything was going so well, she didn't want to take any chances. "Let me think about it a day or two, and I'll get back to you."

"Take as long as you need," replied Steve. "School isn't out for another couple weeks, so we still have time. Just let me know what you decide so I can make an announcement at church. If we're lucky, we'll probably get more kids interested this year."

More? wondered Angela. *Weren't there enough last year?* "Sure, Steve. I'll think about it and let you know."

Angela leaned against the kitchen sink and stared out the window. The birdfeeders were empty. Potholes needed to be filled in the road leading up the ridge. Weeds were popping up all over the cemetery. There were more goats to care for, and Monica had already mentioned growing more vegetables this year. There was so much work to do and so few people to do it. Gilberto was in his eighties, she was turning sixty-five, and Steve and Monica certainly weren't getting any younger. What if she wanted to spend more time down in Alabama with Rebecca and Dominick? Could she just pick up and leave all the work to Monica and Steve? Maybe Camp Gizmo was the only answer.

She picked up the phone to call Steve and heard Pam and Sharon dissecting the latest episode of *As the World Turns.*

"Didja hear what Craig told Lucinda?" asked Sharon.

"Yes, and it's about time," announced Pam. "He should have told her about it when it happened, not a year later. Hey . . . Angela . . . you just pick up?"

"Yes, I was going to call Steve."

"How was your trip?"

"It was wonderful," replied Angela. "Rebecca and Dominick fixed up one of the houses for Gil and me, Dominick raced in his first marathon and took third place, and we all went to a beautiful place called Bellingrath Gardens."

"Well, good," said Pam. "So . . . have you decided about Camp Gizmo yet?"

"How'd you know about that?" asked Angela.

"I was listening when Steve called you."

"Really?" *Was nothing sacred?*

"Of course. How else you think I keep up with things in this holler?"

Angela laughed. She'd been doing a lot more of that lately and it felt good, especially with friends like Pam and Sharon. "You've got a point, there."

"So?" insisted Pam.

"So, yes, I think we'll do the camp again this year."

"Thought you might. Already told my boys."

"And I tol' m'girls," squealed Sharon.

"Then I guess it's a done deal," declared Angela.

"Yup," said Sharon, "but I think you're gonna need a'nudder truck."

"What for?"

"One fer drivin' kids back 'n' forth and one fer haulin' supplies."

"You're probably right," agreed Angela, "but we can't afford another truck right now."

"My cousin, Darrell, up in Reedy has a truck he's been wanting to sell," said Pam. "I think he's only asking two or three hundred for it."

"Two or three hundred? Does it even run?"

"Most of the time," replied Pam.

"Maybe we should look for something more reliable. After all, we wouldn't want to get stuck out on the road somewhere with a bunch of kids jumping around in the back."

"You wouldn't have to take it out on the road," said Pam. "You could just use it on the farm."

"Oh . . . you mean a farm-use truck?"

"Sure," chirped Sharon. "Most everyone has one. They don't have to be registered or licensed or nuttin'. All's you gotta do is put gas in 'em."

"When can we go look at the truck?"

"How's tomorrow?" asked Pam.

"That'll work. I can be at your place after morning chores, and I'll see if Monica wants to come along. She knows a lot more about trucks than I do."

The following morning after the goats were milked and turned out into their play yard, Angela and Monica, accompanied by Steve and Gilberto, rode with Pam to her cousin's farm in Reedy.

Even by West Virginia standards, where everything was just *up the road* or *a stone's throw away,* it took almost two hours to reach the cousin's farm. When they finally arrived, it appeared no one was home. That, however, didn't bother Pam, who slipped on a pair of rubber galoshes, and trailed by her passengers, trudged across the cow pasture where Darrell's truck was parked.

Three cows nibbled the grass around the truck while a bull monitored the situation from the shelter of a huge black walnut tree. Angela and Monica, shocked and perhaps a bit horrified, stood back and anxiously watched as their husbands raced toward the vehicle with what could only be deemed childlike glee.

One of the truck's mud-splattered bumpers lay in the clumpy grass. The other, dented and looking as if it had been through a war, hung on by sheer willpower. All four tires were flat, the top of the rounded cab was crushed, the grill was bashed in, and both doors were open, rusted through and in need of handles. There were no windows, and the upholstery, or what was left of it, was shredded and reincarnated into several large nests.

"Whaddaya think, Gil? Is she a '36 or '37?"

"Neither. She is a 1938."

"How can you tell?"

"The grill is oval. Before 1938, the grills were oblong. And notice the hood? It was the first conventional front-opening truck hood in the industry."

Shaking her head in utter astonishment, Angela turned toward Monica. "1938? That truck is older than me."

"It beats me by almost fifteen years," roared Monica.

Carefully watching where they stepped, the two women made their way through the pasture. As they neared their husbands, they heard them discussing how they would bring the disheveled vehicle back to its former beauty.

"We'll have to check out the brakes," said Steve.

"And the clutch and transmission as well,"

added Gilberto. "Maybe we can buy some used tires from the co-op."

Angela couldn't believe her ears. "You're not thinking about buying this thing . . . are you?"

"Of course," replied both men in unison.

Gilberto stroked the truck's battered hood affectionately. "This is a 1938 Ford half-ton pickup. It has a V-8 engine, a 9.125 inch dry single pressure plate clutch, worm and roller steering, and a completely redesigned bed . . . the first since 1931."

"How come you know so much about it?" scoffed Monica.

A wistful expression spread across Gilberto's face. "I had one just like it when I was Dominick's age."

Angela closed her eyes and nodded. When Gilberto was Dominick's age, he was an orphan supporting four younger sisters. Even though a truck like this one couldn't have cost more than five or six-hundred dollars brand new, Gilberto had probably bought his used. After all, how far could a young waiter's salary stretch? "When was that, Gil?"

"The late 40s . . . 1948 or '49, I think. I was twenty-one years old and needed a truck to take things to my sister who was away in the convent. My truck looked exactly like this one . . . except mine was always clean."

Angela hugged her husband and kissed his cheek. "Thank you," she whispered.

"For what?"

"For being you."

"Does that mean we can buy this truck?"

"And as many more as you can find like it," babbled Angela.

Two days later, after patching the tires and filling them with air, Pam's cousin hooked a chain to the truck's undercarriage and towed it to Steve and Monica's farm. When Steve pulled out his wallet to pay for the truck, Darrell shook his head in protest. "Putchur money away, Preacher. I ain't gonna take nuttin' from the church. Sides, I'm glad to git this thin' outta my field. Them cows was beginnin' to take a shine to it . . . if ya catch my drift."

Steve chuckled and slipped the wallet back into his pocket. "Thank you, Darrell, that's mighty Christian of you."

"Don' knows as I kin be called a Christin' seeing as I ain't been ta church since I were a kid, but maybe God will take kindly ta my act and let me inta Heaven when m'time comes."

Steve rested his hand on Darrell's shoulder. "I'm sure He will, Darrell. You are a fine and upstanding man."

Darrell blushed and shuffled his feet. Then, pulling a well-used handkerchief from his back pocket, blew his noise and turned away. "Gotta run. Dropped the wife off in town 'fore I came out 'cheer, and I gotta pick 'er up 'fore she has a fit."

Gilberto and Steve spent the following week getting the truck back into running order. The engine and clutch were okay, but the brakes, transmission, fuel pump, and radiator all had to be replaced. Running short on funds, they decided to repair the upholstery and windows at a later date and temporarily laid a sheet of plywood over what was left of the bench seat, then covered it with a padded furniture blanket they found in Steve's barn. Although the blanket reeked of cat urine and had holes chewed in several places, it would do until they could afford something better. As for the truck's exterior, they washed away years of grime, Bondoed as many holes as possible, and tried to pop the dents out of the doors and cab. After replacing the bumpers with two-by-fours and attaching secondhand door handles purchased from the local auto parts store, the truck was ready to go. It wasn't pretty, but at least it ran.

Angela stood back and eyed the derelict

vehicle suspiciously. Its once red finish was weather-beaten and pitted and sported patches of some dull gray primer. The words "farm use" were scrawled across both doors in white paint. "Is that thing safe?" she asked.

"I don't know," replied Steve. "Let's go for a ride and find out."

The first thing Angela noticed after crawling into the truck was the hard seat and no seatbelts. "Isn't it against the law to ride without seatbelts?"

"Only if you're out on the open road," replied Steve. "Right now, all we're going to do is cross over the bridge and head up the hill to your place. What can happen?"

Not even trying to hide her fear, Angela braced herself against the dashboard and passenger door. As the truck bounced across the wooden bridge, she looked out the window at the river below. Luckily, the water was nothing more than a stream. If the truck broke down on the bridge and fell into the water, she probably wouldn't drown.

As they started to climb the hill to the top of Hummingbird Ridge, the engine stalled. After several tries, Steve got it started again, but when he engaged first gear, the truck slid backwards. Gunning the engine, he regained control and crept slowly up the hill.

When they reached the ridge, Angela refused to let go. Afraid to move, she didn't even turn her head to face Steve. "This is not a truck," she groused. "It is a Red Devil."

Steve slapped the steering wheel. "You know . . . you're right. And I think that's just about the finest name anyone could come up with. Thanks, Angela."

Angela shot a surly look Steve's way before proceeding to climb out of the truck.

"Wanna come for dinner?" he asked as she walked away.

"Only if I get my stomach back by then," she replied.

Almost twice as many children signed up for Camp Gizmo as the previous year. In order to provide more hungry people with food, several garden plots had been planted in various areas of the farm, and the Red Devil was put to good use. Not only did it carry supplies back and forth between the gardens and the church where the restoration continued, it also came in handy as a moveable lunch wagon, bringing food to the workers instead of them having to come in to be fed.

When the first crops were harvested in

mid-June, the children sold them at the farmer's market and donated the money to buy a new bench seat for the truck. Little Florence, having grown a full six inches over the winter, wasn't in favor of getting rid of the plywood. "I like it the way it is," she whined. "It's like riding on a Ferris wheel." She was, however, overruled by Angela, who refused to sit on a cat and mouse blanket. And soon a just-as-good-as-new brown and yellow plaid seat cushion graced the truck's interior. Unfortunately, a replacement seat-back was unavailable, so the plywood and holey blanket shifted position, and Angela continued to find other ways to get around the farm.

By the last week of June, the church had been painted inside and out, the floor waxed and buffed, and the pews and preacher's perch put in place. All that had to be done was raise the tower and hang the bell in its new home.

The day before the church was scheduled to reopen, Steve and Gilberto, with unsolicited guidance from Monica and Angela, loaded the bell tower, heavy end first, into the Red Devil's cargo area, tied a red T-shirt to the pointy part hanging over the end, and convinced several of the older male camp members to crawl in and keep the 20-foot-long structure from falling out.

Traveling down the road from Steve's farm toward the church didn't present any problem. In fact, except for when they hit a few deep potholes, the boys didn't even have to hold onto the tower. When they started up the steep trail to the church, however, everything changed as the heavy end of the tower started to pull away from the truck cab. Two boys jumped toward the rear of the truck bed and tried to wrestle the structure back into position. Two others screamed at the top of their lungs.

Steve slammed on the brakes, causing the rear end of the truck to rise up off the ground and send the bell tower smashing into the cab. At that same moment, the truck's right front tire dropped into a deep groundhog hole, bringing the truck, its passengers, and the bell tower to an immediate standstill. When Steve tried to rock the tire out of the hole, there was a loud rubbing sound.

"Uh oh," he said. "I think we may have broken an axle."

"Do the tires respond to the steering commands?" asked Gilberto.

"I don't know," moaned Steve. "We're stuck in a hole and nothing is responding to anything. What do we do now?"

"We should get out and look," suggested Gilberto. "Maybe it is nothing more serious than a broken tie rod."

As the two men climbed out of the truck, their wives approached from the bottom of the hill. "What happened?" asked Monica.

"We don't know yet," replied Steve. "Gil was just about to take a look."

The news wasn't good. "It looks like a stabilizer bar has broken," reported Gilberto.

"Can it be fixed?" asked Angela.

"Sì," replied Gilberto, "but today is Saturday and the auto parts store closes at noon. We will not be able to get a replacement until Monday."

"How are we going to get the tower up to the church?" asked Monica.

"The only way we can," proclaimed Steve. "We'll carry it."

By this time, all of the Camp Gizmo kids had gathered around to see what was happening. Although none of them seemed overjoyed about carrying the lanky bell tower, they pulled it from the truck, raised it to their shoulders, and carried it the rest of the way up the hill. Once they reached the church, they removed the red T-shirt, attached two previously positioned *Come Along* winches to the base of the vinyl bell tower, and hoisted it to the church roof where two other boys with pneumatic nail guns sat waiting to secure it in place. Next came the bell.

Angela examined the bell as several children prepared it for the ride to the top of the tower. It was the same bell the children had paid for with money they'd earned last year at the farmer's market, the same bell they'd raised to the top of the old church before the devastating fire, the same bell that had crashed to the ground when J.B.'s still exploded and Angela's brother Tony had finally admitted he was an alcoholic.

A gentle rain, a strange occurrence for an afternoon in West Virginia, began to fall as Angela watched the bell being raised. Lifting her eyes skyward, she remembered a verse from the bible. *Unless a man be born again of water and the Spirit, he cannot enter into the kingdom of God.* Standing in that rain, she felt as if she was witnessing the miracle of rebirth . . . the bell's, the church's, Camp Gizmo's, her own, and maybe even her brother's.

The following morning, as the bell rang out and friends and neighbors packed into the restored church, Angela knew the Spirit was among them.

CHAPTER 18
FIREWORKS

Monica sounded every bit like a stern parochial school principal. "There is no earthly reason you have to hang around here. The goats are doing well and won't need any shots until winter, the gardens are producing bumper crops, and the Camp Gizmo kids are working their little hearts out. And . . . if anyone gets out of line, Florence will whip 'em into shape."

Angela knew her friend was right. There *was* no reason she couldn't spend the Fourth of July in Alabama. With Monica in charge, the goats would be in good hands, literally, and the Camp Gizmo kids were so busy they probably wouldn't even miss her. Rebecca had said there would be fireworks over the bay, a flea market in town, and a barbecue on the beach. The last time she and Gilberto had been in Alabama, the weather had been a little too cool for swimming. Maybe this time they could dive into the bay and get more than their toes wet. Wouldn't that be fun? They could run down there, spend a couple days, and come back relaxed, recharged, and ready to get back to work. All they had to do was jump in the car and go.

"Well . . . if you're sure you won't mind . . ."

"I won't mind," insisted Monica. "Life is short. Just go and have some fun."

After stopping overnight in Chattanooga and allowing Gizmo the opportunity to sniff all the delectable perfumes on the Cumberland Trail, Gilberto and Angela arrived at Mariposa Landing shortly before noon on the third of July. It was a Friday, and Rebecca was attending some sort of town meeting, but Dominick was on hand to welcome them.

"Great timing," he said. "I just got back from training. Got a late start 'cuz I slept in late this morning, so I only did twenty miles. Don't like to push too hard in this heat."

Angela walked alongside her grandson as he rolled toward the small guesthouse he insisted belonged to her. "What time do you think your mom will be home?"

"Said she'd try to be back by one, but you never know with these meetings. With all the going-ons for the Fourth, everyone's gotta get their two cents in. We might not see her for three days."

Dominick unlocked the guesthouse door and pointed toward a new forty-inch television dominating the coffee table. "Bought that with the money I won on Mother's Day."

Angela couldn't believe her eyes. Although the television's black screen was only about four inches deep, it stood a good two feet above the coffee table and covered almost half the window. Standing up, she could still see the bay, but once she sat down on the sea foam green sofa, she knew the tranquil view would disappear. Televisions were nice when there was nothing else to do, but the proximity of the bay was one of the things she loved about being at Mariposa. She considered asking Dominick if the set could be moved, but decided doing so might hurt his feelings. "Oh, Dominick. We really appreciate this, but you shouldn't have spent all your money on us."

"It's okay," he said. "I got more when I came in second at Nor'lins last week."

"New Orleans? I didn't know you were going to race there."

"It was a spur of the moment thing. Some of Jack's old friends organized a half marathon to help raise money to repair homes down there. Did pretty good, too, even though they had to pay the winners."

Dominick's ear-to-ear grin was better than prize money for Angela. Bending down, she hugged his broad shoulders and kissed his cheek. "Thank you for the fabulous gift, Dominick. I'm sure Gil and I will enjoy it."

Dominick leaned his head to one side and wiped his cheek on his shirtsleeve. "Yeah, well, I gotta run. I'm supposed to meet someone at the pier in fifteen minutes."

"Anyone I know?" Angela remembered Rebecca mentioning she was trying to discourage Dominick's relationship with Marisol, his latest girlfriend. According to Rebecca, it wasn't the girl that was a problem, it was her brother and the two men he hung out with . . . the men from the Piggly Wiggly . . . the men from the boat. If Dominick was going to meet Marisol, her brother and his friends might also be there.

"Just some guys," mumbled Dominick as he spun his chair around and wheeled toward the door. "See ya later."

"What was that all about?" about Gilberto.

"Rebecca believes Dominick may have gotten in with a bad crowd, and I'm afraid he's on his way to meet up with them."

"Do you want me to stop him?"

"No," sighed Angela. "It probably wouldn't accomplish anything but make him mad. Besides, I could be wrong."

Angela and Gilberto were sitting on the front porch of their cottage when Rebecca parked her car in front of her house at four-thirty. Waving, she raised the trunk and tugged on a large box.

"Wait," yelled Angela, "we'll give you a hand." Running across the road to Rebecca's car, they arrived just in time to close the trunk.

"It's not heavy," said Rebecca, "it's Chinese. My meeting ran so late I knew I wouldn't have time to make dinner. So instead of taking you someplace noisy, I ordered takeout. You like Chinese . . . don't you?"

"Of course," replied Gilberto as he took the box from Rebecca's hands. "After Italian, it is my favorite food."

"I thought you liked Mexican," teased Angela.

"Well, sì, I like that, too."

"Is there anything you don't like?" asked his wife.

Gilberto's eyes twinkled as he smiled at Angela. "Sì . . . thin gravy and overcooked pasta."

Angela held the door open for her husband and playfully punched his shoulder as he carried the box into Rebecca's house and placed it on the kitchen table. After helping Rebecca set out plates, forks and chopsticks, she started pulling white boxes out of the larger box.

Pointing to each of the boxes, Rebecca identified the contents. "We've got beef with pea pods, Peking Duck, Moo Goo Gai Pan, sweet and sour pork, steamed rice, and spring rolls."

"What?" chuckled Angela. "No fortune cookies?"

Rebecca reached in the box and pulled out a small plastic bag. "I got almond cookies instead. They taste better."

"You are so right," agreed Angela.

Sitting down at the table, Angela glanced out the kitchen window. "Aren't we going to wait for Dominick?"

Rebecca shook her head as she started opening the takeout boxes. "He left a note saying he'd grab something in town."

Angela detected concern in her daughter's voice. "Is everything all right, Rebecca?"

"No, not really," admitted Rebecca. "Dominick's new girlfriend was picked up last week for shoplifting, and I just found out one of her brother's friends has a prison record."

Angela stared at her daughter in silence. She wished she could help, but teenagers were a complete mystery to her.

"I've tried reasoning with him," continued Rebecca, "but everything I say seems to go in one ear and out the other."

"Would you like me to talk to him?" asked Gilberto.

A spark of hope brightened Rebecca's eyes. "Oh, Gilberto, that would be so wonderful. Dominick thinks of you as a grandfather, and he would pay attention to what you have to say. You know . . . man to man."

"It would be my honor," replied Gilberto. "And now, let us eat this wonderful food while it is still hot. Cold Chinese is not nearly as flavorful as cold Italian."

Everyone dug in. While devouring the contents of the white containers, they discussed Rebecca's goats, the upcoming festivities, and the weather, but not Dominick, who never showed his face.

After helping Rebecca clean up the kitchen, Angela suggested taking Gizmo for a walk along the shore. Rebecca begged to be excused, stating she was worn out and just wanted to take a bath and do some reading before going to bed.

Sensing her daughter needed some alone time, Angela kissed her on the cheek and reached for Gilberto's hand. "Come on, Sweetheart, let's go look for seashells."

It was a typical July-in-Alabama evening . . . hot and humid with dark storm clouds forming over the bay. Hurricane season had started a couple of weeks ago. Could these ominous clouds be harbingers of things to come? A bottlenose dolphin broke the surface of the tranquil water in search of air; ambitious seagulls pecked at lethargic hermit crabs; Gizmo ran back and forth with a piece of driftwood clamped tightly between his teeth. Still holding his hand, Angela asked Gilberto what he was going to say to Dominick.

"I do not know," confessed Gilberto. "I spoke before thinking."

They walked in silence for a moment.

"Did you ever think," asked Angela, "that at our age we'd have to worry about how to talk to a teenager?"

Gilberto laughed, let go of Angela's hand, bent down, picked up a smooth stone and skipped it across the water. It bounced ten times before disappearing below the surface. "The world record is fifty-one skips," he muttered distractedly. "I read that in the *Guinness Book of World Records.*"

Angela bent down, picked up a stone, pulled her arm back and aimed for the water. Letting it fly, her stone bounced twelve times. "Maybe you could tell him his mother is worried about the friends he's been making."

"No," said Gilberto. "If he thinks Rebecca has been talking to us about him, he might lose his trust in her."

"That's true, but why else would you be talking to him if she hadn't talked to you first?"

A clap of thunder followed by an intense lightning flash startled Angela. "Wow, that was close. Maybe we should get back before it starts raining."

The second the words were out of her mouth, a large raindrop splashed the top of Angela's head . . . then another . . . and another. Suddenly, the wind picked up and waves began pounding the white sand beach. She called for Gizmo, who already sensing danger, had abandoned his drift-wood and was racing toward her. Quickly clicking the dog's leash in place, she reached for Gilberto's hand, and above the din of torrential rain, yelled, "Let's get outta here."

By the time they reached the front porch of their cottage, Angela, Gilberto, and the dog were soaking wet. "What are we gonna do?" giggled Angela. "We can't go inside and drip all over those beautiful waxed floors. Dominick would have a hissy fit."

"Let us stay here until we are dry," suggested Gilberto pointing to the porch chairs.

Angela turned her head away as Gizmo stood in front of her and shook his body. "That could take a while," she sputtered, picking wet dog hair from her face.

"Sì," agreed Gilberto, "but in the meantime, we could sit here and enjoy the storm without having to be in it."

"Enjoy?"

Gilberto pointed toward the sky. "Look how the clouds roll across each other, amore. And notice how the setting sun is obscured by the darkness but still illuminates the water? Is that not beautiful?"

Angela studied the clouds. Gilberto was right — they were beautiful. But they were also a little frightening. Thankful she had a loving husband to protect her, she pulled the porch chairs closer together and invited him to sit down. Almost dry, Gizmo lay at her feet. She was surrounded by the two most important men in her life. She leaned her head against Gilberto's shoulder and watched as streaks of lightning jumped from the belly of one cloud to another, tracing silvery spider webs across the sky. She closed her eyes and fell into a peaceful, dreamless sleep.

Waking the following morning in the house and in pajamas, she wondered if Gilberto had prepared her for sleep, or if she had done it herself. Realizing it didn't much matter either way, she stretched and looked out the bedroom window. The sun was shining, the birds were singing, and the smell of fresh coffee tickled her nose. It was the beginning of another beautiful day and she didn't want to miss a moment of it.

Jumping out of bed, she tiptoed into the kitchen, slipped her arms around her husband's waist and nuzzled his neck that smelled of soap and shaving cream.

"Sit down and eat your breakfast," scolded Gilberto. "Today is going to be a busy day."

Angela poured herself a cup of coffee and sat at the small dining table. Outside, the bay was once again tranquil, and except for a few weather-beaten branches, all signs of the storm had vanished. "What's on the program?" she asked.

"Rebecca stopped by and said she was on her way to the park to set up for the barbecue."

"Did she say if she needed help?" She stuffed a forkful of scrambled egg into her mouth. It tasted of oregano and garlic.

"No, but she said to make sure we were at the park by three o'clock when the barbecue begins."

"What are we going to do until then?" She forked more egg into her mouth. This time, she tasted cheese. *But what kind? Mozzarella? Swiss? No . . . Fontina.*

"I thought we might go to the flea market," said Gilberto as he sat at the table with a plate of eggs and a cup of coffee.

"Good idea," agreed Angela. "It'll give us a chance to see more of the town and maybe meet some people."

After breakfast, Angela and Gilberto drove to the municipal park, found a parking spot in the almost-filled parking lot, and after slathering themselves with SPF50 sunscreen, began walking around. Since the sun was bright and Angela had forgotten to bring along a hat, Gilberto bought her a blue plastic sun visor with her name and the image of a swallowtail butterfly spray-painted across the broad brim. Not only did the visor keep the sun out of her eyes, it matched the lace-trimmed chambray sundress she was wearing.

While they were checking out a table filled with seashell jewelry, they heard someone calling their names. "Yoo-hoo, Gil . . . Angela . . ." Turning toward the sound, they spotted Vesta Renoux — hard to miss in her hibiscus red muumuu — waving and pushing her way through the crowd. When the woman reached them, she seemed almost euphoric. "Well, fancy meeting you here." She cooled her face with a handheld battery-operated fan. "Looks like it's gonna be a scorcher. Good thing you dressed for the weather. Like your hat, Angela, get it here?"

Angela touched the brim of her hat and nodded. "Why yes, Gil bought it for me. Wasn't that nice?"

"Oh yes, he's just the best, honey, knew that the moment I met him. Y'all going to the fireworks tonight? From what I hear, they're gonna have some real dazzlers — get it? Fireworks? Dazzlers? Well, it sure was good seein' ya again but I gotta run. Jack's got a table down on the shady side of the park where it's nice and cool. If I stand out in this sun any longer, I'm gonna melt. Make sure you come see us, hear?"

As fast as she'd arrived, the flamboyant woman was gone. With a quizzical expression on his face, Gilberto turned to Angela. "How can she talk so fast? She did not even take a breath."

Angela chuckled. "Years of practice, darling, years of practice."

After checking all the tables, but only buying triple scoops of homemade ice cream stuffed into handmade waffle cones, Angela and Gilberto headed for the picnic tables and barbecue area where Rebecca was helping a small group of Cub Scouts set up a lemonade stand. The boys, all about eight or nine years old, seemed intent on batting away all the bees that had gathered since they began setting up.

"No one's gonna buy our lemonade," whined one of the boys.

"Yeah, whatta we do now, Miz Taylor?" moaned another.

Happy to see her mother and father-in-law, Rebecca quickly enlisted their help. Handing them half-filled plastic Coke bottles, she asked them to place the bottles away from the tables but close enough to the stand to lure the bees away from the sugary lemonade. "The bees will be attracted to the scent of the Coke, crawl inside the bottles and drown."

"That's cruel," protested Angela jokingly.

"Maybe so, but it's better than dealing with a pack of bee-stung Cub Scouts."

The Coke bottle trick worked, and the Cub Scouts soon found their drink stand surrounded by a swarm of thirsty people.

Once everything was under control, Rebecca suggesting getting something to eat before the supper crowd arrived. "There's pecan-smoked barbecue, shrimp-on-a-stick, ribs, slaw dogs, chicken wings . . . you name it, we've got it."

Having eaten enough ice cream to sink the USS Alabama, Angela chose the shrimp while Gilberto pigged out on drenched-in-sauce barbecue and spicy fries.

"You're gonna regret that in the morning," cautioned Angela.

"Ahh . . . but tonight I shall feast. Smell this sauce, *amore*. Is it not delectable?"

Instead of just smelling, Angela took a huge bite of Gilberto's sandwich. Wiping sauce from her mouth, she smiled. "Umm . . . wanna trade?"

When the sun started to set, many vendors, already sold out, closed their booths as customers wandered toward the beach. The fireworks wouldn't start until nine, but everyone, especially those who'd been to the display before, wanted to get a choice spot from which to watch the show.

While many people chose the beachfront, Gilberto pointed toward a grass-covered hill. "I believe we will be more comfortable if we go up there."

"He's right," agreed Rebecca. "The grass is softer than the sand, and we won't have to fight off sand fleas."

Gilberto returned to his truck, retrieved two blankets from behind the front seat, and spread them out on the grass. He and Angela shared one blanket, Rebecca sat on the other.

"Is Dominick coming?" asked Angela.

"No," replied Rebecca. "He said fireworks were just for kids and old people. Guess which he thinks we are?"

Angela tried to make light of Rebecca's comment but sensed that, deep down, Dominick's evasion of anything having to do with family was hurting her daughter. Anything that hurt Rebecca, hurt Angela. The bond between mother and daughter was growing stronger, but Dominick's actions might threaten it. Gilberto planned to talk to the boy in the morning. *Would it do any good?* She doubted it.

The fireworks started shortly after nine. Accompanied by a concert of music by Tchaikovsky, Rossini, Sousa, Gershwin, Woody Guthrie, and Julia Ward Howe, red, blue, green, gold, and silver skyrockets, aerial shells, and roman candles lit up the night sky and illumined the darkened water. Angela lay back on the blanket and Gilberto joined her. Rebecca hugged her knees and watched the sky.

Everyone rose when The Star Spangled Banner played. As the fireworks ended, the crowd cheered and then started for home.

Returning to the parking lot after the show, Rebecca noticed her left front tire was flat. "I knew I should have stopped for air," she muttered.

"Do not worry about it now," said Gilberto. "We will drive you home, and I will come back tomorrow and repair the tire."

"Thanks, Gil. I appreciate your help."

The ride back to Mariposa Landing went quickly with discussion of anything important being completely avoided.

Rebecca was the first to see the flashing lights. "ICE."

"Where? What?" Gilberto slammed on the brakes.

"Don't stop," she shrieked. "It's an ICE raid — Immigration and Customs Enforcement. I've got to get in there."

The entrance to the farm was blocked by two local police squad cars. A uniformed officer stepped out of one of the squads, approached Gilberto's truck and demanded to see everyone's identification.

Rebecca handed her driver's license to the officer. "I'm Rebecca Taylor," she said, obviously trying to keep her voice calm. "I run this farm."

The officer looked at the license and then at Rebecca. "Sorry, Miz Taylor, I didn't recognize you."

"What's going on?" she asked as the other squad car pulled away with one person sitting in the backseat.

"ICE agents have been checking farm camps all over the county. They picked up five illegals in Turkey Branch last week."

"But all of my workers are documented," she argued.

"Yeah . . . they found that out."

"So who was in the back of that car that just pulled out?"

"I'm sorry to have to tell you this, Miz Taylor, but, I'm afraid it was your son . . . Dominick."

CHAPTER 19
ALL FOR LOVE

Either half-asleep or totally bored, the booking officer never looked from the paperwork in front of him. "We're charging your son with possession and intent to sell marijuana. Both are felony offenses in Alabama punishable by one to ten years in jail and a maximum fine of $200,000."

Rebecca braced herself against the officer's desk. "Can I see him?"

"Normally, I would say no," replied the indifferent officer, who finally made eye contact with Rebecca. "But seeing as he's only fifteen, I'll give you five minutes. She can go, too," he added, pointing at Angela. "But the man has to stay out here."

Angela, who had been standing with one arm around Rebecca's shoulders, turned around and looked at Gilberto, silently pleading for his approval.

"Go," he said. "Your daughter and grandson need you."

Rebecca and Angela followed the booking officer into an interrogation room where Dominick was being detained. The floor of the room was covered in carpet, the walls were painted a soothing green, and an unbarred window looked out on a small garden. Unlike all the TV cop shows, there were no two-way mirrors, graffiti covered walls, payphones, video cameras, or open-for-all-the-world-to-see toilets.

The boy sat at a long southern pine table with his head buried in his hands. He looked up when Rebecca and Angela entered the room, his handcuffs revealing the enormity of his situation.

Taking a seat directly across from her son, Rebecca reached across the table and laid her hands on top of his. "Tell me what happened."

"I messed up," he mumbled, his face devoid of any emotion.

"Yes, I can see that." Rebecca kept her voice calm, even though she was probably churning inside.

Dominick leaned back in his wheelchair, lowered his chin, and began his story. "After you left for the park, I met up with Raúl and Marisol down at their boat."

"Raúl is Marisol's brother," explained Rebecca.

Having personally met the man, Angela needed no explanation. He was trouble, and if only by association, so was his sister.

"Raúl said he knew of a way we could make some easy money. All I had to do was sneak him onto the farm after the sun went down."

"And what?" asked Rebecca. "Sell marijuana to the innocent farm workers?"

"Some of them aren't so innocent," snapped Dominick. "One guy offered to trade me an old Colt .45 he said his great-grandfather used in the Spanish-American War. You should have seen that thing — it was all shiny and looked like it weighed a ton."

"Quit changing the subject, Dominick. Why were you arrested?"

"Esperanza said her father collected antique guns and the Colt would make a nice Christmas gift for him, but since I didn't have anything to trade I talked Raúl into selling me a kilo of marijuana. Just as the trade was going down, all these bright lights came on, and some dudes on bullhorns started yelling for everyone to drop to their knees and put their hands in the air. Of course, I couldn't drop to my knees, so I just sat there and hoped for the best."

"Were you frightened?" asked Angela.

"That's not the word," replied Dominick. "Let's just say I'll probably have to destroy the jeans I'm wearing when, and *if,* I get home."

"Let me get this straight," said Rebecca. "The only reason you had any marijuana was because Esperanza wanted a gun for her father?"

Dominick hung his head. "I'd do anything for her."

Angela knew love, or what most people thought of as love, could make you do strange things. The first time she'd thought she was in love, she'd thrown caution to the wind and ended up pregnant. Some years later, a smooth-talking man convinced her to move to a farm and work her fingers to the bone, while he ran around and chased other women. The only time being in love turned out well for her was when she fell in love with and married Gilberto. But even then, she'd come close to losing everything because of jealousy. She wanted to console Dominick, but what could she say? She kept quiet and listened as Rebecca tried to sort things out.

"Okay . . . this is what we're going to do. We came straight from the fireworks, and I didn't bring much cash, so I'll have to go home, get my checkbook, then try to find someplace that will cash a check this late at night. I'll try to get you out of here tonight, but if I can't come up with enough money, you might have to wait until after the bank opens in the morning. Since they'll probably want to charge you with a felony, you'll need a good lawyer. Offhand, I don't know of anyone to call but maybe Jack does. I'll talk to him in the morning. In the meantime, do everything you're asked to do and don't mouth off to anyone." Rebecca rose from her chair as the officer unlocked the door and held it open.

Unable to reach out to them, Dominick hung his head as his mother and grandmother rose to leave. "I'm sorry, Mom," he said.

Rebecca bent down and kissed the top of her son's head. "I know you are," she replied. "Just hang in there . . . we're gonna get through this." She hurried away before Dominick could see her tears.

Although it was his first offense, Dominick's bail was set at $50,000, a sum much higher than Rebecca could readily cover with cash. The bail bondsman advised her she could use a credit card to get Dominick out of jail quickly, but opting to practice a little tough love, she decided to let him spend the night there. She told Angela and

Gilberto that the Stapleton jail was known for being clean and treating its inmates well.

"No harm will come to him, and he might learn a valuable lesson." She sounded as if she didn't believe her own words.

The next day, Jack Renoux came up with the name of a lawyer who agreed to represent Dominick and also negotiated to get the boy released on his own recognizance.

When Rebecca and Angela picked Dominick up from the jail, he appeared subdued.

"Have you eaten anything?" asked Rebecca.

He nodded. "They brought breakfast in from the White Gull, but I wasn't very hungry so I just ate the toast."

"Do you want to stop and get something on the way home?"

"No, I'm not feeling very sociable right now. All I want to do is go home, take a shower, and put on some clean clothes."

When they turned into the farm entrance, several workers were standing along the side of the road. A few waved nervously. The man who offered to trade his revolver hung his head.

Angela parked Gilberto's truck next to Dominick's. Before going to the jail, she and Rebecca had dropped Gilberto off at the park so he could fix Rebecca's flat tire.

When he was finished, he would drive Rebecca's truck back to farm.

Dominick got into his wheelchair and headed toward his house. Halfway there, he turned around and faced Rebecca. "I'll make this up to you, Mom," he promised. "I don't know how yet, but I'll find a way." Then he was gone.

Rebecca froze in her tracks and looked skyward. "What should I do, Lord?" she cried. "I know I should be mad at him, but all I want to do is wrap my arms around him and protect him from all the bad things in the world."

Taking her in her arms, Angela allowed Rebecca to cry on her shoulder. She knew what her daughter was feeling, because she was feeling it, too. Maybe sheltering one's child was an instinctive thing — not something that mothers *learned.* "Whatever you do," she told her daughter, "remember that God will be with you."

"I know," sobbed Rebecca, "but sometimes He feels so far away."

Angela had an idea. "He's never farther than the nearest church," she said as she tipped her head toward the farm's church. "Why don't we go inside and talk to Him?"

Rebecca and Angela entered the small white church and sat in the last pew. "I don't like to sit up front," said Rebecca as she dried her tear-stained cheeks. "It seems too presumptuous."

Angela nodded. "So the last shall be first and the first last . . ."

"Do you read the Bible, Mom?" asked Rebecca.

"Not enough," she admitted.

"When I was growing up, my grandmother made me read it every day. 'It is God's Word,' she would tell me. 'Everything you'll ever need to know is in there.' Well, I think my grandmother was wrong, because I don't remember reading anything about a mother protecting her son from harm."

"How can you say that, Rebecca? The Bible tells us that Mary tried to protect Jesus from cradle to death, that Jochebed saved her baby Moses from Pharaoh's death edict, and that Rebecca tried to save Jacob, her favored son, from his brother's wrath. And what about the woman who was ready to give up her baby rather than allow King Solomon to cut it in half?"

Rebecca grinned. "Sounds like you read the Bible a lot more than I do."

"I'm sorry," said Angela. "I didn't mean to preach."

"You weren't preaching, but if you'd like to come back next Sunday, I could set you up with a pulpit and a congregation."

Angela sighed. "It's very peaceful here."

"Yes, you were right about God being here." She reached for Angela's hand.

Angela and Rebecca sat in the last pew of the little white church and silently told God what was in their hearts. They didn't pray out loud, they didn't sing hymns, they didn't fall to their knees. They just communed with their maker.

After about twenty minutes, Rebecca suggested going back to her house for coffee. Angela agreed, and the two women reluctantly left the church.

Upon entering the house, Rebecca called out for Dominick. "Gram's here, Dom. Come and have coffee with us."

No answer.

"Dominick? Are you home?"

Boomer came running, but without Dominick.

Looking out the window, Rebecca noticed her son's truck was still parked next to Gilberto's. Going to the bathroom, she knocked on the door. When there was no response, she opened the door and looked in . . . no Dominick. "Looks like he isn't home," she announced. "I hope he hasn't gone looking for Esperanza or Raul."

"Maybe he went for a run," suggested Angela.

"Of course," agreed Rebecca. "After spending the night in jail he probably needed to get out and stretch his muscles."

Two hours later when Dominick still hadn't returned, Rebecca began to worry. "He's never out this long." Her voice was filled with panic. "I'll call Jack . . . maybe he's with Dominick."

Jack didn't know where Dominick was. "I talked to him a couple of hours ago, but he didn't mention anything about going for a run. Would you like me to go out and look for him?"

"Oh, would you?" whimpered Rebecca. "That would be wonderful."

Gilberto walked into the house and laid Rebecca's car keys on the kitchen table. "I am sorry I took so long," he apologized. "The tire had a large nail in the sidewall, so I decided it was best to replace it." Detecting Angela and Rebecca's distress, he asked what was wrong.

"Dominick is gone and Rebecca is worried he might be looking for Raúl," explained Angela. "Jack is out looking for him, and we were just getting ready to do the same thing."

"I will drive," insisted Gilberto. "Neither

one of you looks calm enough to drive right now. Does Jack have a cell phone?"

"Yes," replied Rebecca. "I have his number stored on my phone."

"Good. Call him and tell him to keep in touch with us while he is searching. That way, we will not search the same areas."

Driving away from the farm, Rebecca caught sight of several of her most trusted farm workers. Asking Gilberto to stop the truck, she told the workers that Dominick was missing and asked if they could help search for him. When they agreed without hesitation, she gave them her cell phone number and told them to call her if they had news. All in all, five groups set out to search for Dominick.

Within ten minutes of leaving the farm, Rebecca received a call from one of her workers. "We have found his baseball cap, Miz Taylor."

"Where?" she pleaded.

"On the old dirt road leading down to the bay."

"I know the road he's talking about," exclaimed Angela.

Rebecca stared at her mother with surprise and confusion. "Show me," she demanded.

Gilberto turned the truck around, raced back to the farm, and followed Angela's detailed directions across the back end of the property. When they reached the dirt road, he slowed down and jockeyed his Super Cab around potholes and across the washboard surface. Angela thought the road had gotten worse since the first time she'd traveled it, but she didn't voice her opinion because to do so would have been to betray Dominick's confidence.

Up ahead, they noticed a truck stuck in the ditch. It belonged to Pedro, the man who found Dominick's cap. "I was talking to my wife, telling her what was happening, and I hit a pothole. Now my tire is flat, and I am stuck in this ditch."

"Do you want us to pull you out?" asked Gilberto.

"No, you go ahead. Just follow those tracks, I believe they were made by Dominick's wheelchair." He pointed to tracks in the red soil.

Rebecca and Angela jumped out of the truck, inspected the tracks and agreed they had been made by Dominick's chair. Calling Jack on the cell phone, Rebecca told him about the tracks and asked him to help pull Pedro's truck out of the ditch. Then Gilberto drove rapidly toward the bay.

Just beyond a clump of trees, they spotted Dominick struggling to maneuver his wheelchair up the hill leading from the bay. Something large and brown was spread across his lap. When they got close enough to make out the object, they realized it was Gizmo.

Gilberto jerked the truck to an abrupt halt as Angela and Rebecca unhooked their seatbelts and got ready to jump out.

"Come help Gizmo," yelled Dominick. "He was attacked by an alligator. I think he's dying."

After helping Rebecca check Dominick for injuries, Angela dropped to her knees and examined her dog. Both of the dog's front legs bore deep gashes, his right ear was pasted against his blood-soaked head, and his jaw dangled loosely. "What happened?" she wailed.

"I wanted some fresh air," began Dominick, "and when I went outside and heard Gizmo barking, I decided to take him along for company. Since I didn't know how he would react out on the open road, I headed for the bay."

"Were you looking for Raúl?" asked Rebecca.

"Sorta," admitted Dominick. "I figured maybe if I talked to him, he'd tell the cops the stuff was his."

"Didn't the police tell you to stay away

from him?" questioned Rebecca.

"Well, yeah, but . . ."

"We need to get Gizmo to a vet," shrieked Angela. What would she do if something happened to the dog? He was part of her life, almost as important to her as her husband.

Gilberto lifted the limp dog from Dominick's lap and carried him to the truck. Angela jumped in through the passenger door and laid a blanket across the seat, bunching one end into a pillow for her dog's battered head. Following his wife's instructions, Gilberto laid Gizmo on the blanket, then Angela crawled in next to the dog as Rebecca and Dominick climbed into the truck bed and prepared for a bumpy ride.

While waiting as a veterinarian worked on Gizmo, Dominick filled in the gory details of the alligator attack. "When we got down to the bay, no one was around, but I thought I saw something moving in the water so I moved in closer to see what it was. Gizmo must have spotted it, too, because he kind of got in front of me and started growling . . . real mean like. I tried to get him to move out of the way, when all of a sudden, this giant alligator jumps out of the water and lunges toward us." The boy was talking with his hands almost as much as with words. Someone, probably his mother, had found a couple of Band-Aids and placed them on his scraped knuckles.

"Gizmo never flinched. He jumped that 'gator and started biting for all he was worth, but the alligator turned around, grabbed his two front legs, and chomped down."

Angela gasped and buried her head in Gilberto's chest.

"I grabbed a stick and tried beating the alligator over the head, but it only made him madder. He let loose of Gizmo and lunged toward me. That's when Gizmo bit its head and got it turned away from me."

"That creature could have killed you," uttered Rebecca.

"I wasn't worried about me," snapped Dominick. "I was worried about Gizmo."

"Even so . . ." objected Angela.

The veterinarian, a woman in her late forties, entered the room. It had been almost three hours since she'd begun work on Gizmo and she appeared exhausted but hopeful. "I wired his jaw and reattached his ear; the wounds on his legs were superficial; and there was no obvious bone damage. Everything looks good, but we'll have to watch out for infection. If it's all right with you, I'd like to keep Gizmo overnight for observation."

Angela and Gilberto nodded their heads. "Of course."

"He's sedated now but you can go in and say good-night if you wish."

Angela followed the veterinarian toward the operating room door but turned around before reaching it. "Dominick? Would you like to come, too?"

"Sure," he answered.

Angela and Gilberto patted the sedated dog's head and inspected his bandages. Healing was going to be a long process, but they were confident their dog would pull through.

Before leaving, Dominick leaned forward and kissed Gizmo's forehead. "Get well quick, big guy, I love you."

Angela sniffled as she shuffled out of the room.

Two days later, Gizmo was back on his feet, and, even with a wired jaw, acting as if nothing had happened. It was time to head back to West Virginia but Angela was reluctant to leave. "I wish we could stay longer," she told Rebecca. "But I promised Monica I'd hurry back to help her with the canning and Gilberto told Steve he'd help with the second hay harvest."

"I know," replied Rebecca, "there's always

something to do on a farm."

Dominick rushed up and handed Angela a paper bag. "This is for Gizmo," he said. Angela reached inside the bag and pulled out a stuffed toy. "What on earth . . . ?

"It's an alligator," said Dominick. "One that won't bite."

Even though leaving was sad, Angela was happy. She had her family, she had her dog . . . all seemed right in her world.

CHAPTER 20
JOIE DE VIVRE

She didn't feel old, she didn't act old, and looking in a mirror, Angela didn't think she looked old. Yet, here it was — September 12th — her birthday — and she had just turned sixty-five. By some standards, that meant she *was* old.

Where had the years gone?

It seemed like only yesterday she was growing up in Indiana, trying to keep out of trouble and constantly bickering with her brother. During her high school years she'd vacillated between thinking she was too fat, too skinny, too shy, or too bold. Those were good years, but then she'd gotten married, only to find out marriage didn't necessarily mean living happily ever after. After her divorce, everything had gone steadily downhill. In fact, just a couple of years ago, she'd felt as if she had hit bottom. She had no friends, a crummy job, and the prospect of nothing good ever happening in her life.

When her landlord essentially evicted her, it was like having a door slammed in her face. But as someone once said, when God closes a door, He opens a window. That window was Gilberto, her loyal friend, her loving husband, the world's best cook.

She raised her nose in the air and sniffed. Strange . . . she couldn't smell a thing. Normally, by the time she got up, Gilberto had started breakfast, and truth be known, it was the smell of whatever he was cooking that woke her. If nothing else, she should at least have been smelling coffee.

Slipping into a chenille robe to help ward off the early morning chill, she tiptoed, barefooted, down the stairs and toward the kitchen. Maybe, if she were quiet, she could sneak up and surprise her husband.

No Gilberto, no pans cooking on the stove, just a note on the table:

Amore, I have gone to town to run errands. I will be back around noon. Do not worry about Gizmo as I have taken him with me. Ciao, Gil.

Well, there it was. He hadn't fixed breakfast, he ran off without asking if she needed anything from town, and he had taken her dog with him. She was all alone in the house . . . on her birthday.

Since cold cereal didn't sound particularly appetizing, she skipped breakfast, took a quick shower, and got dressed. Maybe she would grab a bite with Monica after they finished with the goats.

Walking down the hill to Steve and Monica's farm, she thought about the things she might do on her special day. She could milk the goats, of course, spend time with Steve and Monica, call her dear friend, Gelah, stop at Pam's house when she walked down to get the mail, and then what? Clean the house? Do some sewing? Bake herself a cake? *No.* Today was her birthday and she was going to have fun.

When she reached the goat shed, she found another note:

Hi Angela, Sorry I'm not here to help with the goats, but Steve and I had to go to town with Gil. Be back when we get back. Luv ya, Monica.

What was going on? Her husband and friends had gone off without her, and as for the notes . . . neither one even *mentioned* her birthday. Had everyone forgotten?

While milking Sophia, a thought came to her. Why not go to town and have a day of pampering? She could have her hair done, get a manicure, and maybe even spring for a facial. Then, instead of just calling Gelah, she could take her out to lunch. It would be a sort of "Girls day off." Sixty-five? Eat your heart out, Ferris Bueller.

It was already ten o'clock when she finished with the goats. By the time she called Gelah and washed up, it would be after eleven. That didn't leave much time for pampering. Maybe they would just have lunch and go shopping instead. She could even look for a new pair of winter gloves. After all, her old ones were on their last legs, and as every good goat herder knows, warm hands are welcome hands.

Calling Gelah proved fruitless. There was no answer, and since the older woman didn't have an answering machine, she couldn't even leave a message. That's all right, she thought. There's always Pam.

But Pam wasn't home, either. Neither was Sharon when she called her house. *Where was everyone?*

Like it or not, Angela was on her own. Back in the old days, that thought might have sent her plummeting into the dumps. But now, every day — no matter what it brought — was an adventure, an opportunity to discover something new, a chance to make new friends, an occasion to celebrate the joy of being alive. She would have lunch at the new Victorian tearoom that had just opened in town and then go looking for those gloves.

Although unusual for a small farm town, the tearoom turned out to be an excellent choice. The street-facing windows were covered in lace panels; the six round tables were dressed in mauve linen; a single bud vase holding a sprig of baby's breath and a pale pink rose graced each table.

When Angela walked in, the restaurant had been completely empty. Choosing a table near one of the windows, she watched what little traffic there was pass by. By the time the waitress brought a menu, three other women had walked in. Two sat at a table in the back, the third stood at the door, looking around as if trying to decide whether or not to stay.

Laying her menu on the table, Angela waved at the woman, who looking a bit puzzled, walked up to the window table.

"Do I know ya?" asked the woman.

Angela stood and offered her hand. "No," she replied. "My name is Angela Fontero and today is my sixty-fifth birthday. Would you like to join me for lunch?"

The woman smiled shyly, accepted Angela's invitation, and sat down at the table. "My name is Hattie Morgan," she said looking around nervously. "I never bin in a place like this a 'fore. What kinda food ya think they serve?"

"Probably small sandwiches and salads," said Angela. "Do you want to look at the menu?"

The woman shook her head. "Cain't read," she admitted. "Never made it past the third grade."

Hattie Morgan appeared to be about Angela's age, maybe a year or two older. It was hard to tell because farm life was hard on West Virginian women. They had little education, they worked long hours, and they got little, if any, reward.

Realizing the woman might not know the difference between a savory and a scone even if she could read the menu, Angela asked, "Why don't we just ask the waitress to bring us today's special and see what we end up with?"

"Good idea," agreed Hattie.

The special of the day consisted of raisin scones with lemon curd, cream cheese and cucumber finger-sandwiches, chicken and gorgonzola salad, and three different types of tea — all for ten dollars per person. During lunch, the women compared notes about their farms, their husbands, their children, and their grandchildren. Hattie had five children and twelve grandchildren.

When it came time for dessert, the waitress placed two decadent French pastries, one with a candle, on the table. "I heard you mention it was your birthday," she said. "This is compliments of the house."

Angela blushed. "Thank you very much, I wasn't expecting this."

The women ate their pastries, paid their lunch tabs, exchanged telephone numbers, and agreed to get together again soon. They had met as strangers but parted as friends.

While walking toward the department store to see if they had winter gloves in stock yet, Angela considered all the things for which she was thankful. She had her health, she had her faith, and most importantly, she had her family and friends.

For starters, there was Gilberto, the man who stood by her, laughed at her jokes and never criticized her cooking. About as perfect as a man could be, he was her rock, the one she could count on, the one she could go to in good times and bad, the one who brought Rebecca and Dominick into her life.

Her daughter — two words that had always been in her heart but were seldom spoken. In her lifetime, Rebecca had suffered many hardships, yet she'd risen above them, and instead of feeling sorry for herself, reached out to help less fortunate people. If God had offered Angela a choice of daughters, she would have picked Rebecca.

Dominick. Now there was a surprise. Not having a clue about what to do with him, Angela was sure she could never again live without him. Like his mother's, his life had been difficult, but he didn't let anything hold him back and he never played the pity card. A few months ago, some ill-chosen friends and a kilo of marijuana had threatened his future. Fortunately, an understanding judge looked into the matter and decided a change of friends and probation would be punishment enough for the boy. Since then, Dominick was doing everything in his power to vindicate himself. From what Rebecca had told her mother, he'd accomplished that ten times over.

Not only had Angela's friends Steve and Monica gotten her back on the straight and narrow path, they had invited her into their lives, given her and Gilberto a home in which to live, and held her hand whenever it needed holding. For all that they were, and all that they had done, they held a special place in Angela's heart.

And then there was Katherine — crazy, unpredictable, outrageous Katherine. She had yanked Angela out of her protective shell, shown her an exciting new world, and then pushed her headfirst into it. If it hadn't have been for Katherine, Angela might be sitting in some lonely room, staring at a television, and waiting for the final bell to ring. Instead, she was enjoying her life as a wife, mother, grandmother, and tattooed goat farmer.

Angela found her gloves, bought an extra pair for Monica, and headed for home. When she reached the top of the ridge, she saw Gilberto's truck. Rushing inside the house to tell him all about her eventful day, she discovered it was empty. No Gilberto, no Gizmo . . . just another note:

Come down to the river . . . everyone is waiting.

What was going on? Who was waiting? Who had written the note? It certainly wasn't in Gilberto's handwriting.

Angela laid her packages on the kitchen table, ran upstairs to the bathroom to freshen up and comb her hair, then tore out the door and down the hill. Maybe Gilberto and her friends had remembered after all. Maybe they had even planned a little party.

Before reaching the river, Angela noticed a large white tent with several pickup trucks parked haphazardly around it. It hadn't been there when she went down to milk the goats earlier that morning. Maybe that was what Steve had gone to town to get. Maybe he was holding a Revival. But if so, why hadn't he asked for her help?

As she got closer, she heard music. Definitely not the soul-jerking gospel songs played at a Revival — this was *dancin'* music. And, as if to prove the point, J.B. was clogging on a wooden platform set up under the tent.

Katherine was the first to spot Angela. Jumping up and down, she screamed at the top of her lungs, "Surprise."

Angela froze in her tracks as the group gathered beneath the tent rushed toward her. Neighbors, friends, family . . . they were *all* there. They had *all* remembered. Tears coursed down her face as they broke into song.

Happy birthday to you, happy birthday to you, happy birthday dear Angela, happy birthday to you. And many mooooore.

Katherine grabbed Angela and hugged tightly. "Happy birthday, sweetie. Guess what? Mongo and I are gonna move back . . . isn't that great?"

Pam and Sharon kissed Angela's cheeks. J.B. shook her hand. Gelah dried her tears with a crochet-bordered handkerchief.

When Steve announced it was *Party Time,* everybody rushed back to the tent where Monica was frantically uncovering the casseroles and bean pots the women had prepared. In the middle of a paper-clothed table stood a three-tier birthday cake covered in delicate pink frosting and adorned with tiny pink rosebuds.

"I made that," said Widow Putnam, the woman Angela had once made soup for. "Hope ya likes it."

Dominick rolled across the rocky soil with a beautifully wrapped box on his lap. "There was a race in Atlanta this weekend," he said, "but I told all the guys I'd rather spend it with my grandmother. Happy birthday, Grams."

Accepting the box, Angela stuck it under one arm, bent down and planted a juicy kiss in the middle of her grandson's forehead.

Pretending to be embarrassed, Dominick hung his head, then looked up and grinned at Angela.

Tony elbowed his way through the crowd surrounding his sister, hugged her and whispered in her ear, "I've been sober for ten months. Thanks for showing me the way, Sis."

Angela looked around and realized the only things in life that truly mattered were family, faith, and friends — and she had them all! They were what made getting up in the morning worthwhile. They were what

327

gave her life meaning. They were what brought joy and hope into her life. She felt like leaping in the air, clicking her heels and shouting God's praises to the sky.

So she did.

MESSAGE FROM ANGELA

Hi Everyone,

Well, there you have it . . . my life in three small books. I know some of you might not think there was anything extraordinary about it, but after all, isn't life just a string of ordinary day-to-day events all run together into one big, beautiful tapestry? Sort of like Gelah's Circle of Life . . . everything and everyone is related in one way or another. I guess it's up to each one of us to seek out those relationships and complete our own circle.

I wish to thank all of you who have contacted me. Your encouragement, comments, and advice was greatly appreciated. Having my story put down on paper was cathartic, even if some of the situations were tweaked to make them a bit more interesting.

Many people asked if the characters in my books were real. Let me put it this way . . . although most of the individuals in the books were created in the mind of my author, some were based on real people I have known and loved . . . and they know who they are. Thanks, guys!

One thing I need to point out is that, as you undoubtedly noticed in this last book, several references were made to things such as shrimp fishing, trawlers, and white sand beaches. Since all three books were written retrospectively, what was once true is no longer.

The catastrophic Deepwater Horizon oil spill in the Gulf of Mexico in 2010 drastically changed the scenery and quality of life in the Gulf Coast region. Pristine beaches were defiled, wetlands and estuaries contaminated, birds and sea life endangered (some species may never recover), businesses closed, jobs were lost and lives, my own included, were dramatically impacted. When I am up to talking about what has happened, I will tell everything to Margaret who may — or may not — decide to write another book.

Until then, dear friends, remember that no matter how old or young you are, life is all about joy, hope, and new beginnings with family, friends and strangers. Also remember that you don't quit playing because you grow old . . . you grow old because you quit playing.

Go out and do something fun and exciting, be kind to one another and say a prayer for all those who suffer.

I love you all . . .

ANGELA

P.S. As always, you can email me at angeladunn08@aol.com.

The employees of Thorndike Press hope you have enjoyed this Large Print book. All our Thorndike, Wheeler, and Kennebec Large Print titles are designed for easy reading, and all our books are made to last. Other Thorndike Press Large Print books are available at your library, through selected bookstores, or directly from us.

For information about titles, please call:
   (800) 223-1244

or visit our Web site at:
   http://gale.cengage.com/thorndike

To share your comments, please write:
   Publisher
   Thorndike Press
   10 Water St., Suite 310
   Waterville, ME 04901